1

Novels by Kelly Cheek

All We Hold Dear
Trial by Fire
The Lost Colony
JackSimile and the Phantom Fury
Spirit Breather
The Piper

The SpiritSense Series
In Restless Dreams
First Light
When We Were Gone Astray
Gazing Into the Abyss
Undying Love
Snow Angels
A Life Worth Living
Black Heart
Black Candles

The Facebook Trilogy
Profile
Private Messages
Poked

BLACK CANDLES

Kelly Cheek

Cover and book design by Kelly Cheek

ISBN: 979-8-9899039-4-8

Printed in the United States of America

I have now decided that my death should be very precious. I really want to use it. I'd like my death to be as interesting as my life has been, and will be.

—David Bowie

Three men waded purposefully through the tall saw grass under a full moon.

One, Terry, a geeky-looking man in his early thirties, bore a backpack and a belt full of assorted items — an array of electronic gadgetry, meters, etc. He considered himself to be the voice of reason, especially when things got a little dicey, and the others insisted on continuing. His voice of reason usually involved sarcasm delivered with an inflection which, to his dismay, was often quivering in those dicey moments, and usually didn't get the results he hoped for. His suggestions were seldom heeded.

The second man, James, was a few years older. His olive skin, dark hair and dark eyes gave him an exotic look, though he hailed from Wisconsin. He carried a video camera on his shoulder. He was brave enough to keep the camera rolling no matter what was happening, and usually without commentary. He spoke occasionally from behind the camera if he felt it was important. He always kept the camera aimed, primarily, on the third man.

The third man, who was actually the leader of the group, was a bit of an anomaly. A well-known ghost hunter, he was in his fifties, with long greying hair pulled back into a low ponytail. Sporting a greying beard which was trimmed, but often a little ragged, his face had a lived-in look. He had an athletic build, wearing a shirt with the sleeves torn off. His bare muscular arms each bore tattooed sleeves of intricate, detailed images, which included many paranormal and occult representations.

As the trio continued across the field toward the forest, the bearded man looked up, and his baritone voice could be heard over the sound of their footsteps and the swishing of the saw grass against their waders.

"The full moon, wrapped wraithlike in its misty swaddling of clouds, backed away, cautiously keeping its distance from the intrepid traveler who strode persistently toward it."

"That moon seems like a pretty smart cookie," said Terry, the man carrying the backpack. A slight palpitation could be heard in his voice. "So, tell me, why are we going *into* the forest?"

The leader looked at him with a crooked smile, his eyes a little wild.

"Because that's where the ghosts are!"

The forest closed over them, blocking out the brilliance of the moon. The only illumination, now, was the artificial light shining from the camera.

» § «

An ancient cypress tree was the primary focus of the trio. The ground was soggy, but the area was not flooded. The tree was surrounded by trinkets and artifacts of all kinds. Dolls and flower arrangements and arrows and small bottles of liquor. And even money.

They were accompanied by a constant chorus of insects, frogs in a nearby pond, and nocturnal birds.

"What's that?" James calmly asked from behind the camera. "Can you hear that?"

The other two turned to him questioningly.

"It's like a persistent whispering," he explained.

They all strained to hear it, but it wasn't entirely audible, particularly over the drone of natural sounds. In the end, James admitted it could have just been a breeze blowing through the cypress needles.

"It's freezing!" Terry said, shivering, his attention diverted from whatever James heard.

"It's barely Spring," Ponytail said with a crooked smile.

"Yeah, but we're in southern Florida, asshole," Terry retorted. The leader grinned at him, obviously unconcerned about the verbal slight. "You do remember just ten minutes ago it was seventy degrees?" Terry looked down at his kestrel meter. "It's forty-two here."

"Well, then, I guess this must be the place," their leader replied with a deep, resonant voice that sounded almost serene.

"Okay," he said, turning toward the camera, "here's the story." His voice was pitched lower, now, but still loud enough to be picked up on his clipped mic. "In late 1865, John Dixon arrived in Florida from Charleston. He had just spent the last four years of his life defending his home from the Yankees. He was disillusioned at the outcome of the war, and wanted to get as far away from the Union states as possible.

"He purchased a claim here, near the Everglades, built himself a little cabin, and proceeded to spend his life sulking over the war and bemoaning his wasted years. He became a regular fixture in the tavern that used to stand a mile or so west of here in Tallahoochie, which also no longer exists. He could often be found regaling whoever would listen with his tales of fighting the Yankees.

"His accounts also, quite often, included stories that gave a certain indication of his prejudice against the Native Americans. Many Indians fought in the Civil War, on both sides. Admittedly, that often had more to do with their nearly futile hopes of retaining some portion of their tribal land than with any political investment in either side of the war.

"By the time the Civil War started, the Trail of Tears and other Indian removal schemes had already been done. But one tribe managed to thwart the United States' efforts to remove them.

"The war between the Seminoles and the US Army consisted of three primary conflicts, and all combined, lasted from 1817 to 1858. But though it was one of the costliest and deadliest of conflicts, it ultimately remained largely unresolved.

"By the end, many surviving Seminoles, those who hadn't been killed, or moved to 'Indian Territory,'" he made air quotes for that, "in Oklahoma, fled into southern Florida, in the Everglades, and the Army basically gave up. To this day, the Florida Seminoles refer to themselves as the Unconquered People.

"By the time the Civil War started, the Florida Seminole people had had enough of war with the white man. They were tired of fighting against them, and they certainly couldn't imagine fighting alongside them. They didn't join the war.

"Based on some of the stories he told, that seemed to be, at least, part of what John Dixon didn't like about the Seminole tribe. However, he seemed to support similar views about Black people and other Indian tribes, including some who actually fought for the Confederacy, so it's been concluded that his expressions were simple bigotry, and had little, if anything, to do with any deeper ideologies or political partisanship.

"But here's the thing." He cleared his throat, more as a pause for effect than a physical need. "A few months into 1866, local people started disappearing. Law enforcement in Tallahoochie was a little tenuous at best, so it took a while for them to start noticing any kind of pattern. When they did, they realized that the missing people were mostly Seminoles, along with a few other Native Americans, a couple of Black people, and even one former Union soldier who was visiting the area.

"Sometime in 1870, somebody had the idea to check around John Dixon's place, and what they found shocked the little community. Numerous shallow graves scraped into the soggy ground, primarily around this tree," he gestured toward the cypress behind him, "contained the bodies of all those missing people. Every individual who had been reported missing was now accounted for.

"One who was *not* accounted for," he paused, again for effect, his eyebrows raised, "was John Dixon. He fled into the swamp, never to be heard from again. To this day, people seek out this tree, whether to commune with those who lost their lives here, to memorialize them, or just out of simple curiosity."

James panned the camera across the base of the cypress tree, and at all the offerings scattered around the spreading knobby "knees" of its roots.

"Some say that the ghosts of those murder victims can still be found in the vicinity of this tree. A few have also claimed to have seen John Dixon here, presiding over his collection of souls."

James focused in on a close-up of his face, one eyebrow raised in what he called his, "Coincidence? I think not" expression. It just made James think of Mr. Spock.

» § «

Vaguely Native American-shaped, a nebulous entity swirled in front of them, elevated near the base of the tree, as the ghost hunter spoke to it, his deep voice entreating in a pleading, reasoning tone.

"Toogojah," he said, "your bodies have been found, and now, your story is told." He didn't reveal that their story had been known for years before now. "You have no need to stay here in this realm. You can move on to the next plane."

He raised his arms in a dramatic, pleading gesture.

"Go and join your people. Your time here is done."

James had moved to a position that actually showed the tear in the ghost hunter's eye.

The entity turned its head to look at all three of the men in the party, and Terry visibly shivered when its gaze fell upon him. It looked back at the ghost hunter, and its demeanor seemed to express something like acceptance and gratitude.

Its head inclined in a relaxed position, and gave a slow nod. Within seconds, the entity flared into a bright flash and disappeared.

» § «

The setting changed as the ghost hunter relaxed in an easy chair in what looked like the interior of a medieval castle. Directly behind him were arranged numerous stone crosses and other grave markings from centuries past.

He took a sip of Scotch and sighed as he set the glass down on a small table next to his chair.

"Thanks to our intervention, the ghosts of Tallahoochie have seen the light," he grinned at his joke, "and they've moved on to the next plane of existence. They've been able to join their friends and family, no longer tied to this earthly realm.

"To those who make the pilgrimage to the John Dixon cypress tree, your services are no longer needed. The souls are free."

He took another sip of his Scotch.

"And to all of you," he looked pointedly into the camera, "join us next time on *King of the Dead*. I'm Damien Specter."

It must be you," Suzy said quietly.

Suzy stood beside Julie's crib, her index finger grasped by the baby. As the child slept, her pacifier pumped up and down in her mouth.

It took a moment for Fin to be able to pull his eyes away from his daughter sleeping in her crib. When he finally did, he looked at Suzy, his eyebrows drawn together in a confused frown.

"What must be me?" he asked quietly. He took the opportunity to look back down at the baby as Suzy gathered her thoughts.

"I know I'm incredibly flawed," she finally replied. "So, it must be you that made Julie so perfect."

Fin raised an eyebrow as he looked back at his wife.

"Me?" he challenged.

"Emma was perfect, too, though," Suzy added thoughtfully, her tone somewhat baffled.

Fin smiled.

"Not to take anything away from your late husband, Mark, but it seems to me that you're the common denominator here."

Suzy looked up at Fin, not responding to his smile. Instead, expressions of doubt and concern were etched across her face as she seriously considered her response. Finally, she shook her head.

"I've been such a mess for months."

"You've been *pregnant* for months," Fin interjected. "And it wasn't an easy one. You've had valid worries about being pregnant in your forties, you've had hormonal issues, you've had supernatural distractions. I think that's enough to make anybody a mess. But, through all of that, you're still perfect."

"Pfft," Suzy scoffed.

"Now, shut up," Fin said with a smile before Suzy could expand on her comment, "or you'll wake Julie."

At the sound of the baby's name, Suzy's train of thought was derailed, and she looked back down at their daughter. The baby had been born a few weeks before, and she lay there now in her crib, her arms up, her hands gripped into tight little fists beside her head, the left one around Suzy's finger, the pacifier moving up and down irregularly.

"Come on," Fin said quietly, gently prodding Suzy to come with him out of the nursery. Suzy gave one last look at Julie and sighed. She carefully pulled her finger out of the baby's grasp, then made sure that the monitor was on. She looked up at Fin and nodded.

She gently closed the door as they left. They went into their bedroom, next to the nursery. She looked at the monitor on her bedside table to be sure it was receiving, and that all was quiet.

"Do you remember when you greeted me at the door wearing your Wonder Woman costume?" Fin asked. Suzy looked at Fin who had plopped down on the bed, one ankle crossed over the other. She rolled her eyes, but she smiled and nodded. "That was one of the most perfect and super-lative moments in my life," he said.

Suzy stared at him in disbelief. Fin disregarded her expression and continued.

"When I saw you then, you looked so sexy and beautiful and strong . . . and perfect. And that moment has defined how I have seen you ever since."

"Bullshit," Suzy scoffed.

"No," Fin replied, undeterred. "It's absolutely not bull-shit. That's not to say that there haven't been problems. There always will be. That's to be expected. But through it all, you continue to be incredibly sexy and beautiful and strong, and perfect," Suzy bristled at the word. "For me," Fin added. "You're perfect for me."

As usual, his adding those two words made the compliment more palatable for Suzy.

Not that he didn't still believe the previous version of the statement.

Suzy looked at him for several moments, her entire demeanor awash in disbelief.

"Don't look at me with that tone of face," Fin said with a grin. "Come here."

He scooted over and Suzy couldn't resist. She joined him, snuggling against his side, her head resting on his shoulder.

"I'm only here because of your clever wordplay," she insisted.

"I know," Fin replied. "And I'm only here because of this expansion project you've got going on." He maneuvered both of his hands so that they could cup her enlarged breasts.

"Oh my god," Suzy said. "These things would never fit in that Wonder Woman costume now!"

"That's okay," Fin replied, nuzzling her ear, his voice soft and deep. "Your birthday suit is my favorite, anyway."

2

Suzy and Fin smiled as they watched Rachel holding and cuddling Julie. Rachel, Suzy's long-time best friend, was visiting for dinner. She lived in Boston, but she and Suzy got together regularly, and over the past several months, the baby seemed to have taken a liking to her, as well.

Now that dinner was over, they were relaxing in the family room at the back of the house. Ursula, their Pomeranian, was curled up between Suzy and Fin. They usually made it a point to engage the little dog whenever Julie was getting attention.

Visible through the large west-facing windows, mainland Marblehead, Massachusetts sparkled across the harbor. The late summer sun was slipping toward the horizon, and the seaside town shone in high contrast with the long shadows.

"Oh, Suzy," Rachel effused, "she's so adorable, she makes my ovaries ache."

A smartass remark immediately came to mind, but Suzy held it in check, knowing Rachel's romantic history. She was nearly the same age as Suzy but had never found "the one."

They thought it might have happened a year and a half ago at Suzy and Fin's wedding. Rachel, Suzy's Maid of Honor, and Jeff, Fin's Best Man, had taken to each other at the time but, unfortunately, it didn't last.

"She gets that from me," Suzy said. "Sorry about your ovaries."

It wasn't callous like the remark that first came to mind, but it was Suzy, and Rachel smiled in response.

Suzy glanced at Fin who nodded slightly. Suzy turned back to Rachel.

"Listen," she said in a tone that dragged Rachel's attention away from Julie, "Fin and I have been talking."

Rachel frowned as she focused on Suzy's serious expression and tone of voice.

"If you're okay with it," Suzy continued, "we'd like for you to have custody of Julie if anything ever happens to both of us."

Rachel's eyes instantly filled with tears. She looked down at Julie in her lap and the tears rolled down her cheeks. She looked back up at Suzy and Fin and smiled.

"You guys, I can't even tell you how honored I would be!"

"Okay, good," Suzy smiled, "we'll make it official."

Rachel looked back down at Julie and raised her voice to baby talk pitch.

"Did you hear that, Julie? I get to keep you! You want to come home with Auntie Rachel?"

Julie smiled and blew a bubble.

"Uh, you realize we have to be dead first, right?" Fin asked.

"Oh, yeah," Rachel said in a nonchalant tone, shrugging her shoulders. She turned back to Julie and used the baby voice again. "Won't you just be the best little consolation prize!"

Julie smiled again, but her eyes were drooping.

"Your smartassery is coming along very nicely," Suzy said admiringly as she stood up.

She took the drowsy baby from Rachel and quietly carried Julie upstairs to the nursery, making cooing sounds at her that were very counter-smartass. Rachel looked down at Ursula, who had jumped down from the sofa, and was sitting at her feet looking up expectantly. She had taken a liking to Rachel, as well.

"Oh, Ursula, of course, I haven't forgotten about you," Rachel said, leaning forward and picking up the little dog. She looked up at Fin.

"What about Ursula? Can I have her, too?"

Fin smiled but shook his head.

"Sorry, our neighbors, Art and Terri, already have dibs on her."

Rachel made a disappointed face and went back to petting Ursula. Fin watched for a few moments from his chair, sipping his whisky.

"I don't know if I ever told you," he said, "but I'm sorry you and Jeff didn't work out." It had been a year since she broke up with him, and he felt guilty that so much time had passed.

Rachel looked at him, while holding Ursula snuggly against her chest.

"Thanks, Fin," she said. She looked away for a moment, pondering her reply. "I hated to call it off," she finally said. "He's a really sweet guy." She thought for a few more seconds. "We just didn't click completely."

"Yeah," Fin replied. He chuckled as he thought about his friendship with the man. "Anybody close to Jeff needs to have a really weak olfactory system."

Jeff's presence was always accompanied by the scent of his favorite cologne, which Fin secretly suspected that he bathed in.

Rachel grinned, then pressed her face against Ursula's soft fur.

"It wasn't just that." She looked up at Fin. "It didn't help, though."

She spent a few moments scratching Ursula's ears and under her collar. Fin smiled as he watched the dog's obvious enjoyment of the attention, occasionally accompanied by a spontaneously scratching hind leg.

He looked up as Suzy came back into the room, the baby monitor in one hand, her phone in the other. The phone had the bulk of her attention. Fin noticed that she had a puzzled expression on her face.

"Suzy?" he said. "What's the matter?"

"I just got a call about a sendoff," she replied.

"Well, that's cool," Fin replied. "We haven't had one in several months." He turned his head, looking at her askance as he watched her face. "What's the problem?"

"It was Damien Specter."

"Damien Specter?" Fin echoed. "The *King of the Dead* guy?"

Suzy nodded.

"I love him!" Rachel said. Fin and Suzy both looked at her, a little mystified. "What?" Rachel responded, looking back and forth at both of them. "You guys are the ones that got me interested in that kind of stuff."

"What did he want?" Fin asked, drawing his attention back to Suzy.

"He needs our help."

3

Rachel sat in the back seat of Fin's Mustang Mach-E, directly behind him, frequently looking at Julie strapped into the car seat on her right. The baby was sleeping, so she wasn't bothered by the shadows of the crisscrossing girders of the Piscataqua River Bridge which were rapidly sweeping down across her through the sunroof and the passenger's window. Looking out the window, Rachel saw the green sign announcing that they were no longer in New Hampshire.

"Welcome to Maine," she said. Then, with a grin, she added, "Are we there yet?"

Suzy and Fin both snickered.

"Sorry," Fin said. "Maine's a pretty big state. We've still got about two and a half hours ahead of us."

Suzy turned from the front passenger seat and smiled at her, acknowledging her joke.

"Do you suppose Damien Specter is his real name?" Fin asked with a glance at Suzy.

"It's not," Rachel volunteered. "His real name is Ronald Herbert."

"Ronald Herbert?" Fin repeated with a grin.

"Got something against pseudonyms, Mikey?" Suzy asked with a teasing edge to her voice.

Fin's smile faded. As an author, Fin had taken on the pseudonym Michael Jones. In more recent years, he had thought, with some regret, of a few names that he wished he had taken that didn't sound quite so generic. Damien Specter would definitely make the list.

"No," he replied quietly. A few moments passed before he continued a little grudgingly. "I have to admit, though, that Damien Specter is a pretty cool pseudonym for a ghost hunter."

"You mean specter hunter?" Suzy asked.

"Well yeah, but not just that," Fin said. He glanced at Suzy again. "Didn't you ever see *The Omen*?"

Suzy scowled at him.

"The horror movie? No!"

Fin nodded. He remembered that Suzy just wasn't into scary movies.

"Damien was the name of the little boy in the movie, the Antichrist."

"Ah," Suzy replied. That was enough for her, and she had nothing more to say about it.

After a few moments, though, she looked at him.

"I hope you're not implying that you think that Damien Specter is the Antichrist."

"What?" Fin glanced at her, his eyebrows pulled together in a frown. "No, I think it's a cool name for the host of a paranormal TV show." He looked at her again. "You know I'm not religious anymore. Why would you think I still believed in something like an Antichrist?"

"Okay, okay," Suzy replied, putting her hands up in a gesture of mock surrender. "Just wanted to be sure."

"If you two lovebirds are finished," Rachel said, "you might be interested to know that Damien Specter lives in Bangor, Maine because he's such a huge fan of Stephen King. Apparently, Damien was a writer before he became the King of the Dead."

"Huh," Suzy replied, "I'm not sure if that qualifies as a fan or a stalker."

She looked back at Rachel and saw the look on her face. Rachel really was a fan.

"We're just joking around," she said, knowing that her sarcastic sense of humor wasn't appreciated by everyone. Fin loved it and dished out as much as she did, but Rachel wasn't always receptive to it. She nodded in response now and smiled. With that encouragement, Suzy, apparently, couldn't quit.

"You know, I had a stalker once. This writer in Colorado moved out here to New England because he was such a 'huge fan.'" She did air quotes.

"I'm your *biggest* fan, babe," Fin confirmed.

He reached over and squeezed her knee. Suzy placed her hand on his, and they ended up with their fingers interlaced.

Rachel looked at their hands and smiled. She turned and looked out the window and sighed.

» § «

Maybe coming with them wasn't a good idea, Rachel thought. The timing had been perfect. They were driving up there early on Saturday morning, spending a few hours meeting with Damien Specter on Saturday afternoon and evening, then coming back on Sunday. She'd be back to work on Monday.

But now, she was reminded why she didn't spend a lot of time with Fin and Suzy. She met Suzy fairly regularly for lunch, dinner, afternoon tea, or whatever, but only occasionally was it with Fin. Their latest bombshell about wanting her to take Julie notwithstanding, it was just getting to be too difficult to see them together.

Suzy and Fin were so suited for each other. They were obviously in love, a perfect match if Rachel ever saw one. She was beyond happy for her best friend, but spending too much time with the two of them was difficult.

Rachel wanted so badly to find someone who would fill that place in her heart, as Fin did for Suzy. For a while, she thought that Jeff might be that one.

But he was such a "guy."

Rachel had long been a fan of the humor columnist Dave Barry, and she clearly remembered a column he wrote years ago about Men vs. Guys. He wrote that, while men accomplish important things like creating art and building monuments, guys like "neat stuff" and "pointless challenges," like super powerful computers and bungee jumping. It was silly humor, but she recognized a certain amount of accuracy and truth in it.

And she realized that, in this context, Jeff was definitely a guy. Rachel wanted a man, a person who could communicate with her using more than Tim Allen-style grunts. Someone who could actually be concerned with how she felt and what she wanted, and who would be determined to at least try to provide it, to the best of his ability. Someone who would be available to her despite whatever sport happened to be in season.

She wanted someone like Fin. But she hadn't found anyone else like him.

It's not that she wanted him specifically. She wasn't attracted to Fin. She was attracted to what he provided for Suzy, and she wanted that for herself.

She was actually attracted to Damien Specter. Now there was a man! Handsome in a rugged way, but intelligent and well-spoken. Bravely willing to march into scary situations to help out people in distress. Knowledgeable about historical and current events and able to draw valid conclusions based on available information.

Rachel had no illusions that Damien Specter would be attracted to her, though she did make it a point to see that her makeup was perfect, and that she was dressed in one of her most attractive outfits.

She actually wondered if she had overdone it. Suzy had looked a little surprised when she showed up at their house attired in a swishy dress for which she had received multiple compliments in the past. It came to her mid-thigh, and given the chilly morning temperature in Bangor, she wore a pair of black legging that managed to showcase her shapely legs. She knew the outfit hugged her curves in a very pleasing way.

Fin had given her a once-over and caught his breath, quickly looking away. After that, he seemed to purposely avoid looking too long at her. She had no intention of trying to seduce Fin away from Suzy, but she smiled inwardly at the effect her looks had on a man. It boded well, she thought, for her chances with Damien.

To be honest, though, she had to admit that she really didn't know much about Damien. Despite the persona he gave off in the show, he lived a very private life.

She realized that she didn't even know if he was married or single. Or gay or straight.

And she belatedly hoped that she wasn't coming off as desperate.

She glanced at Fin and Suzy's hands again, and she smiled a bittersweet smile, happy for them, longing for herself. She clasped her own hands together, turned and watched the miles and miles of trees passing by.

4

When they arrived in Bangor, Fin's guidance system instructed him to get off of I-95 at Hammond Street. They drove for a while through a neighborhood with widely-spaced wood frame houses. Each of them was easily a century old, though well cared for, and surrounded by generous lawns and old growth trees.

Eventually, the old houses changed to old brick-and-mortar businesses. Fin turned right onto Main Street and immediately started looking for a place to park. He found a space about a block past their destination.

They had made one stop on their way, so they could use the restroom, and so that Suzy could nurse and cuddle Julie. The baby fell back to sleep as they got back on the road, gripping Rachel's finger, and had slept for nearly the whole drive.

They walked along Main Street surrounded by nineteenth-century brick buildings. Bathed in bright sunshine, the temperature was slowly rising, but Rachel was glad she had opted for the leggings.

"So," Fin said, "why are we not meeting him at his home-slash-studio?"

"I don't know," Suzy replied. She was pushing the baby carrier/stroller in front of her. "This is what he asked for, but he didn't say why."

"If he needs help with a ghost," Rachel posited, "maybe he wants to tell you about it in a neutral place, without interference or interruption."

"That could be," Fin nodded. "Good point."

A few more steps brought them to an intersection, and Fin saw their destination ahead of them in a line of old brick storefronts set diagonally on the block, with a brick-paved square in front.

"PenobsCoffee," he said. "Cute." The Penobscot River was just a couple of blocks away, here in Penobscot County.

As they went inside, they were engulfed by the rich smell of coffee, and the usual coffee shop sounds, the hissing of the espresso machine, the slightly edgy indie music piped over the speakers, and the somewhat chaotic drone of people talking.

As Fin looked around the dining area, he saw Damien Specter wave at them. He was sitting alone at a table, guarding the three empty chairs around it.

Suzy and Rachel told Fin what they wanted, and he went to the counter while they approached the celebrity ghost hunter. Suzy parked the baby carrier beside the table while Rachel took off her jacket.

"You must be Suzy," Damien said, standing and stretching his hand toward Suzy.

"You recognize me?" she asked, a little surprised, as she reached across the table and shook his hand.

"No," he replied, "you're the one with the baby." He laughed a deep, good-natured laugh and turned to Rachel. "And you must be the friend, Rachel." He held his hand out toward her. "It's so nice to meet you," he said warmly, enclosing her hand in both of his. His eyes traveled appreciatively down her body, pausing noticeably here and there, then back up, ending with a deep and meaningful look into her eyes.

"Thank you," Rachel said, trying not to act as starstruck as she felt. Having practically felt his eyes caressing her body, she decided that she had made the right choice in outfits.

Suzy noticed his look and narrowed her eyelids, but she decided to allow time for him to prove himself. Rachel really did look particularly hot, so she decided that she couldn't really blame him very much for looking.

"Please sit," he said, motioning toward the empty chairs. "I'm Damien Specter. Thank you so much for agreeing to connect here."

"It's very nice to meet you, Damien," Suzy said. She and Rachel settled into chairs, leaving the one between them open for Fin. Rachel glanced to her left at Damien Specter sitting only inches away from her. She looked around, swallowed nervously, then looked back at him.

He was wearing his signature sleeveless shirt, showing off the tattooed sleeves on his arms. He had a denim jacket slung over the back of his chair.

Up close and in person, she could see that his long greying hair was actually almost an equal mixture of dark brown and white hairs. His beard was a little neater than it usually looked in his TV show, when he was out in the field, and his eyes were bluer than she ever realized.

They spent a few moments getting settled while Suzy held Julie who had stirred upon entering the noise of the coffee shop. After rocking her a couple of minutes, the baby drifted off again, and Suzy carefully replaced her in the baby carrier.

"I'm so glad you could join them," Damien said, leaning toward Rachel.

"I am too!" she enthused. "I'm such a huge fan!" She cringed inwardly at her obvious fangirling, but Damien just smiled. He seemed to enjoy the attention. He kept his eyes on Rachel, appreciating the view once again. She couldn't help but smile back at him.

He stood back up as Fin approached the table. He stretched his hand out toward him, then he tilted his head as he looked at Fin.

"You look like—" He brought his eyebrows together thoughtfully. "Aren't you Michael Jones?"

Fin smiled as he shook Damien's hand.

"Fin MacKinley. And aren't you Ronald Herbert?"

Damien laughed good-naturedly.

"Touché. It's good to meet you, Fin."

"You, too." They sat down and engaged in small talk until a barista called Fin's name from the counter. He excused himself and went to get their drinks and pastries, then returned to the table.

"So," Suzy said, getting down to business, "why do you need our help?"

Damien took a sip of his coffee, and the brief grimace that crossed his face indicated that the cup that he had been nursing for however long before they arrived was probably getting cold.

"I have a problem," he said. "One that I don't have any experience with."

"Okay," Suzy replied, raising her eyebrows curiously, expectantly. A few more moments passed before Damien continued.

"I have a brain tumor."

The others looked at him, their mouths open, their faces expressing sadness and shock and sympathy. Fin finally spoke up.

"God, that really sucks, man," he said. "And as much as I think we all sympathize," he looked at Suzy and then at Rachel, who had tears in her eyes, "that sort of thing is not really in our particular wheelhouse, either."

"No," Damien smiled, "I don't suppose it is." He spent a few moments fiddling with his cup, turning it a few times on the table. He took a deep breath and continued. "I've been told that this kind of tumor is inoperable and resistant to chemo and radiation." He looked up at the others. "I have six months or less. And since I don't want to spend my last few months on earth in pain and confusion, I've decided to end my life on my own terms."

"You can do that?" Fin asked.

"I can," Damien nodded. "Based on the 'Death with Dignity Act,' passed a few years ago, physician-assisted suicide is legal in Maine, as long as the patient is terminal, with six months or less to live, and is capable of administering the lethal drug themselves."

Fin and the others sat there looking at him, seemingly in shock. Finally, Suzy managed to get a bit of a grasp on her words.

"Like Fin so eloquently said, 'that really sucks,' but," she frowned, "at the risk of sounding like a heartless asshole, what does that have to do with us?"

"Okay," Damien said. He leaned forward, getting past the darkness of his revelation, gearing up to excitedly reveal his plan, as if he were discussing a heist or a jailbreak. "The part that involves you is that I'm being bedeviled by an evil spirit."

Suzy and Fin both sat back in their chairs, their mouths hanging open as they looked at Damien. Fin's earlier revelation to Suzy about the cinematic significance of Damien's first name came back to them.

"Huh," Suzy finally said. "Also not something we have any experience with." She squinted and glanced at Fin. "I don't think." She looked back at Damien. "I mean we *have* dealt with ghosts who had, shall we say, less than favorable intentions and wanted to kill us." Damien narrowed his eyelids and shook his head. "Okay, what exactly do you mean by 'evil spirit'?"

Damien sighed and sat back in his chair.

"I don't know, a demon from Hell?"

"That sounds oddly religious, coming from you," Suzy observed.

Damien tilted an eyebrow and shrugged.

"Several years of Catholic school before my mother converted to Judaism to marry my stepfather. Some things never completely go away."

Fin frowned at him.

"Pardon my observation," he said, gathering his thoughts, "but you seem strangely unconcerned about the seriousness of this claim."

"Oh, I'm concerned," Damien insisted. "Not for me, though. I'm going to be entering the spirit realm myself pretty soon, and will, hopefully, be able to deal with it on somewhat even ground. And assuming that I can 'go into the light' right away, I may not have to deal with it at all.

"But I'm concerned about leaving my family at its mercies."

"Your family?" Rachel asked. Damien didn't seem to notice the slight hitch in her voice, though Suzy heard it.

"Yes," he replied. "It's a man's God-given responsibility to take care of his family, and Claire," he sighed and shook his head, "Claire is so young and inexperienced with this sort of thing. I think she'd be an easy mark. And my daughter Shannon's a wonderful girl, but I do know that she doesn't really believe in the supernatural, which leaves her wide open to this demon's menace, as well."

"Your own daughter doesn't believe in the supernatural?" Fin asked.

"Well," Damien replied uncertainly, "I can't say we've discussed it in depth, but I know she doesn't really believe in what I do." Damien looked at the others at the table and gave a shrug and a grin. "For good reason."

old up there, Barnum," Fin said. "What do you mean, 'for good reason'?" He tilted his head and looked askance at him. "Are you saying what I think you're saying?"

Damien glanced at each of them, a look of amusement on his face.

"Really?" he replied. He leaned forward and lowered his voice lest nearby customers hear him. "Come on, most of us are fakes to some extent." He snickered and shook his head. "I *am* a ghost hunter, that's for real. But my show is highly rated, not because I'm such a great spiritist, but because of my keen showmanship, my sense of humor, and my eloquent narration."

"Eloquent narration?" Suzy asked.

"Yeah, that's what I call it. I was a writer before I started doing this. I wanted to be the next Stephen King. The eloquent narration is something I do on the show to kind of up the drama or set the stage."

He turned his eyes upward as if looking for inspiration. He turned his gaze toward Rachel and pitched his voice a little lower.

"The gust of wind rushed in an audible path headlong through the forest like a fearsome ghost, untethered by time or place, on a heinous mission to haunt his next unsuspecting victim." He looked back at them, returning to his normal voice. "That sort of thing."

Rachel, her eyes wide as she held his gaze, tried to hide a shiver.

"Huh," Fin said. "I used to do something like that myself. Any that I thought were good, I'd write down for possible use in a book."

"You used to do it?" Damien asked. "You don't any-more?"

Fin shook his head.

"Suzy thought it was kind of weird." He looked point-edly at Damien. "I'm beginning to think that maybe she had a point."

Damien expelled an irritated sigh.

"I also assemble and deliver a lot of historical back-ground. So, besides the excitement of the ghost hunt and ex-pulsion, viewers also actually learn something from my show."

"But I thought you were the real thing," Rachel said, re-gaining some of her composure, her voice drenched in dis-appointment. Damien looked at her, his face, at least, a little regretful.

"I am," he insisted. "But it's not like I can have a one hun-dred percent success rate."

Suzy peered at him with a look of irritation hanging heavily from her face.

"Are you telling me that the sendoffs you do on your show are fraudulent?"

"Sendoffs? Is that what you call them?" Damien shrugged. "I don't know. I mean no. Most of them seem to be real, but we definitely boost the visual effects." He leaned forward in an appealing posture. "We have done follow-ups and found that the ghosts, at least in most cases, do seem to have stayed gone."

He looked at each of them and put his hands up in some-thing of a pleading gesture.

"Come on, it's just showbiz."

Fin glanced at Suzy and saw a bit of a sneer on her face.

"We're not in showbiz," she said.

"Exactly!" Damien replied. "And that's why you're here." He looked back and forth between Suzy and Fin. "You guys seem to be the real deal. And that's exactly what I need."

After spending a couple of minutes on the other side of the coffee shop in an angry impromptu conference, Fin and Suzy returned to the table. Suzy noticed that Rachel seemed a little uncomfortable, and she briefly regretted not including her in the conference, even though she had nothing to do with SpiritSense, the deep and intuitive connection to the spirit world that she, and Fin to an extent, possessed and made use of.

"Okay, Damien," Fin said, "tell us about this 'evil spirit.' Where did it come from?"

"I have no idea," Damien replied, sitting back in his chair and looking at them a little surprised.

"No idea?" Suzy echoed. "You mean to tell me that you can't even piece together a possible scenario as to where this demon came from and why it attached itself to you, of all people?"

"No, none at all," Damien insisted. He looked thoughtful for a moment and then sighed. "I've racked my brain about this for years. I can't figure out how I picked it up. I'm sorry."

"Wait," Fin said, "years? How long has this demon been an issue for you?"

"I don't know, five, six years."

"You can't think of a single 'case' you had," Suzy said, making sarcastic air quotes, "that might have resulted in this spirit attaching itself to you?"

"*King of the Dead* has only been on TV for three seasons. It can't have anything to do with that."

"Well," Fin said, "I assume you were a ghost hunter before you started doing your show. What about cases you had before the show started?"

"I didn't really have any cases before that. I didn't have a ghost hunting business. I didn't freelance or anything like that. Remember? I was a writer. I mean I knew I had this ability, which made itself known at various times, but I never really pursued it before the show."

Fin and Suzy cast a glance at each other, but it was Rachel who jerked their attention back.

"If you're so concerned about what this spirit might do to your family," she said, "then why are you sitting here with us?"

Damien smiled at Rachel, touching her hand briefly, then looked at Fin and Suzy, including them all in his intense attention.

"A little while back, I did some research, and I bought an old grimoire," he looked back and forth at Fin and Suzy, sitting forward again, "you know, a book of ancient spells and invocations."

"Yeah," Suzy replied impatiently, "we all know what a grimoire is." Rachel looked a little confused, but Damien didn't notice.

"Okay," he continued, "so I placed a binding spell on the spirit."

"A binding spell?" Fin echoed. "Are you serious? What is this, Hogwarts?" He looked at Suzy. "Are binding spells really a thing?"

Suzy shook her head and shrugged.

"It seems to be helping," Damien said.

"Then why do you need us?" Fin asked.

Damien looked at him as if he were an idiot.

"What happens when I die?" he asked. "I don't know how these spells work. If I'm not here anymore, will the spell be broken? Will the demon attach itself to my family? Will it start harassing them?"

"Come on, Damien," Suzy said, "a demon from Hell? I mean that's just something from horror movies and church services."

Damien smiled.

"That's exactly what they want you to think. If you don't believe in them, then you have no defenses against them, and then they've got you." He snickered and shook his head. "You can't fight something you don't believe in, and then they have free rein."

Fin tried to hide the shiver he felt.

"Okay," he said, "tell us about this spirit. What has it done? How has it harassed you?"

Damien sighed as he thought.

"So many things," he said, his face reflecting the struggle that he had endured. "Including an absolute abundance of physical temptations. . ."

Rachel, her eyes trained on him, noticed the lightning-fast shift of his eyes toward her. She could almost feel her nipples respond.

"Oh, come on," Suzy protested, obviously catching that same eye movement. "The Devil made you do it? You're blaming a demon for the fact that you're just a goddam horndog?"

"It's not just that," Damien insisted defensively. "There have been other things."

He drew in a deep breath as he remembered.

"Okay, I've had things thrown at me, I've felt the demon's fingers around my throat. Power outages for no apparent reason. One time, I narrowly escaped getting crushed by a heavy bookcase that just happened to tip over all by itself."

Suzy remembered a certain incident involving spontaneously flying kitchen utensils and some potentially deadly Toll House cookie dough in her own kitchen a year or so before.

But that hadn't been a demon, only a vengeful ghost.

"So, is it here with you now?" Fin asked. "Is it bound to your house, to you, or what?"

"The binding spell seems to have confined it to the house," Damien replied, "as well as preventing it from doing anything truly destructive."

Fin shook his head and sat forward.

"I don't know," he said. "From what you've described, it doesn't sound particularly demonic to me."

"And you know all about demonic activity?" Damien asked. His tone was a little sharper than it had been previously, and he looked immediately regretful.

"I know a fair amount from my previous life," Fin replied, "which I'm not going to get into now. But the things that have been *plaguing* you don't seem much different from other hauntings we've heard about or dealt with."

"It *feels* different," Damien said.

"Oh," Fin said, drawing out the syllable sarcastically. "Well, as long as we're basing these findings on something as solid and reliable as feelings."

Damien narrowed his eyes at Fin.

"Don't your feelings ever come into your cases? Don't you ever rely on gut reactions?"

"Occasionally," Fin replied. "Usually, though, we rely on experience, and what we know works."

"I do the same thing," Damien retorted. "And that experience, my knowledge of 'what works,' is frequently added to by reacting to what I feel is right in the moment."

Rachel, and even Suzy, shifted a little nervously in their chairs at the building tension between the men.

"And if it doesn't work," Fin said, "just add some special effects."

"Listen—" Damien's angry response was cut short when Suzy placed a hand on Fin's wrist, and Rachel tentatively did the same with his own. He took a deep breath and nodded.

"I want the damn thing gone," he said. "I don't want to risk leaving any trace of it here to harass my family."

Fin sighed and sat back.

He glanced at Suzy, both of them shaking their heads.

"So, what do you expect us to do?" Suzy asked.

"I'm hoping you can help me send it packing in two months."

"Two months?" Fin frowned at him. "That sounds—oddly specific."

"I want to do it on the air," Damien said. The angry tone was gone, and his excitement returned. "It'll be my finale, the last episode of *King of the Dead*. Unlike most of my shows, it'll be almost entirely unscripted, since I don't know what will happen after I'm gone. I'm hoping that I'll be able to make contact with one of you after I've crossed the veil, let you know what's going on with the demon, and with me."

The smug look on his face made Fin think he was talking about scoring a big-name celebrity guest, rather than killing himself on the air and then attempting to go one-on-one with a demon.

"Either way," Damien concluded, "I think it will be a real ratings grabber. I want to go out with a bang!"

kay, let me get this straight, Einstein." Fin was regarding Damien through slitted eyelids with an expression that indicated that he thought the man was bonkers. "You want to televise your suicide on national TV while one of us is paving the way for you by battling a 'demon,'" more air quotes, "which you have temporarily confined with a binding spell from an ancient grimoire you found at Amazon."

"Exactly!" Damien replied. "Well, except for the Amazon part. The book came from a private individual who sold it to me at an absolutely outlandish price."

"And you're telling me that none of this sounds the least bit out of the ordinary to you?" Suzy asked, looking skeptically at him, wearing pretty much the same facial expression as Fin.

"It sounds *very* out of the ordinary," Damien said with a self-satisfied look of pride on his face. He sat up a little straighter, letting the pride flow through him. "Name any other show that has done anything like that!"

"Excuse my incredulity," Fin said, "but you seem strangely unconcerned about the whole idea of publicly killing yourself."

Damien shook his head.

"I don't *want* to die, but I know I'm going to. I also don't want to spend weeks or months in torturous agony waiting for death to end it. At least this way, I'll be meeting death on my own terms, in my own time. I'll be making my own finale, and in the process, I'll make an episode that will likely break all viewing and sponsorship records, leaving a legacy and a fortune that will take care of my family for the rest of their lives."

Fin and Suzy looked at him for a moment, then glanced at each other.

"Well," Suzy admitted, a tone of reluctance in her voice, "you've actually managed to make this psychotic idea of yours sound just a little less batshit crazy."

Fin regarded him a while longer. Finally, he sat back in his chair, took a deep breath and blew it out, sounding particularly annoyed.

"Alright," he said shaking his head, "not that we're agreeing to this fiasco, but tell us how you see this going down."

"Okay," Damien said, leaning forward again, excited that they were willing to listen. "Unlike my other episodes, where I'm out on location, this whole episode will take place in my home studio." He glanced back and forth at Suzy and Fin. "It's where I do all my sign-offs at the end of each episode."

Suzy shook her head.

"Sorry," she said, "we haven't seen the show."

"Oh," Damien replied, a fleeting look of disappointment in his eyes.

"I've seen it," Rachel said, catching that look. The dejection on his face engendered a surge in her feeling of sympathy for him. "I'm a DeadWatcher." She turned to Suzy and Fin. "That's what his fans are called. It's a really cool set. I was actually hoping we would be meeting there today."

"Well, we can certainly go there," Damien said, looking back at Suzy and Fin. "I'd like to, in fact, so you can kind of get the lay of the land, maybe picture yourself in the setting."

"So," Fin said, pulling the conversation back on track, "we're in your home studio, the cameras are rolling. Then what happens?"

"Okay, I'll start the show by telling viewers that it will be the last episode, and why. I'll introduce you or Suzy, whichever one of you chooses to do it. But I'm cool with you both being there, too. In fact, that would be even better, having the complete SpiritSense team onsite.

"It'll be a really cool crossover, *King of the Dead* and the SpiritSensors. Maybe you can get some more business out of this. In fact," his eyes widened with excitement, "who knows, maybe after I'm gone, you can even develop a show of your own, a spinoff. Based on the ratings that I know this will generate, I'll bet you could name your price and the production company will gladly give it without blinking."

Fin and Suzy exchanged a noncommittal glance. Damien saw the look and nodded, ruefully dialing down his enthusiasm a little.

"Okay, maybe that's something we can talk about later." He took a calming breath and continued. "I'll talk a little bit about the evil spirit, the kind of shit it's done, and what I hope to accomplish in having you there. I'm thinking we might join forces and try to oust the demon before I take the drugs, but if we can't, then I'll try to assist you from the other side.

"I already have the medication. I'm not sure what it is. I think it might be a lethal dose of morphine or something like that, but they don't tell you what it is.

"Anyway, when we feel like we've done enough of the setup, and we think it's time, I'll take the medication, my body will die, and then I'll make contact with you from the other side. At that point, hopefully, we can expel the evil spirit by working on it from both the physical and the spiritual sides in tandem."

"And if we can't make contact with you?" Suzy asked. She thought about her conversation with her dead daughter, Emma, several months before. "I've learned that time works a little differently on the other side."

"In that case, I'll have a prerecorded message prepared in advance, which they can add in post-production, if necessary." He took a deep breath, as if coming down from his adrenaline rush. "At any rate, I want you there and the cameras rolling until the lights go out. Until I'm dead and gone. Hopefully I *will* be able to make contact and provide a real and conclusive ending to the story, sending that fucking demon back to hell."

Rachel was the one who responded.

"We'll make sure that your family is taken care of."

I'm sorry," Rachel said contritely from the back seat of Fin's car, Julie's little fist wrapped around her index finger. "I didn't mean to speak for you."

"It's okay," Suzy replied. "Nothing's been signed. We're under no obligation."

They were following Damien eastward out of town, the Penobscot River on their right, as he led the way in his 1964 Dodge 330. He had bragged about the car before they left the coffee shop. Years ago, the car had been labeled the "most evil car in America." Damien likened it to Stephen King's *Christine*.

According to numerous stories, the car had originally been a police cruiser. During this time, according to the legend, three different police officers drove it, and each ended up killing their families and then themselves.

Its next owner reported that the car would spontaneously open its doors and jam the steering wheel when she was driving it on the highway. Obviously, this proved to be troublesome for her.

During this owner's 'possession,' members of a local church heard the stories about the car's notoriety, drew their own conclusions as to the source of its un-carlike behavior, and vandalized it. Not long afterwards, several of the vandals were decapitated in a fatal confrontation with a semi.

After that, there was a child who did nothing more than touch the car and then, supposedly, killed his entire family. According to the legend, this was enough for members of a *different* church to chop the car up into little pieces and scatter the pieces to different junk yards.

Damien didn't say whether the car had been reassembled, or if the legends were just that, urban legends. Or if it was simply another 1964 Dodge 330.

"Let me get this straight," Suzy had said sarcastically, before they left the coffee shop. "You're driving this killer car around, but you just can't figure out where your demon might have come from?"

"I bought the car over ten years ago," Damien had replied. He shook his head, smiled and shrugged.

"So," Suzy said now, looking at Fin as they followed behind Damien, "what do you think about his plan?"

Fin glanced at Suzy, then back at the road. He looked out his window at the beautiful and sprawling cemetery they were passing, and Suzy got the impression he was hesitant to answer. Finally, though, he did.

"I think the guy is a crackpot." He paused but Suzy could sense a hesitation, and she waited. "I have to admit I'm a little scared, though," he sighed. "And I know it goes back to my own past life among my hyper-religious family and friends, so it's likely that it's simply a lingering bit of religious superstition, just like Damien's."

"How does this case relate to your religious background?" Rachel asked. She didn't know as much about his past as Suzy did.

"They believe that evil spirits, demons, are those angels who turned away from God millennia ago and threw in their lot with Satan. They're extraordinarily powerful, immortal, superhuman creatures, not the somewhat pathetic entities sometimes portrayed in movies. I mean those are initially scary or else there wouldn't be much of a movie. But they can usually be dispatched through something within the human's power."

He paused for a moment to gather his rambling, disconcerting thoughts.

"There's a verse in Isaiah that tells about a single angel killing 185,000 Assyrian soldiers in one night. So, if you believe that sort of thing, the—the stories, the mythology, the doctrine, whatever, then this is not a creature that would end up being vulnerable to a special gun, or some kind of explosion, or a cross and some holy water. The *only* thing that can defeat a demon is absolute faith and reliance on God."

He allowed a couple more seconds to pass before continuing.

"But they also believe that our spirit doesn't survive the death of the body, that when the body dies, the soul dies, and that's it, until God resurrects us. And, considering that belief, in cases where there have been actual confirmed reports of ghosts, then these are demons, as well, rather than disembodied spirits. So, as one SpiritSensor to another," he shrugged, "I admit they may not be the last word on what this evil spirit really is.

"Since then, I've taken a bit more . . . evidence-based view of things. Still, I lived with those beliefs my whole life, before I started questioning things, so that bit of anxiety I'm feeling is very likely related to that. Old habits, and beliefs, are hard to break."

"That makes sense," Rachel said. "Something that was a part of you for so much of your life is bound to have a lasting effect."

Fin glanced at her in the rear-view mirror, seeing the understanding in her eyes, and he nodded.

Following Damien, Fin turned onto an older, narrow road. The paving, while mostly intact, seemed decades older than the road they left, and was, in places, cracked and bumpy. The maples and pines were much closer to the sides of the road here. A few of the maples were just starting to change color, and combined with the pines, they darkened the drive.

After a few minutes, they turned off the road onto a gravel drive, which was narrower, and the trees pressed even closer to them. Fin slowed a bit and backed away from

Damien's car to keep from getting his paint or windshield nicked by flying gravel.

A mile or so later, the trees parted away from the road a little, and finally opened into a large clearing revealing a great stone wall.

The gravel road led toward a pair of enormous wooden gates, which began swinging inward as they approached, likely controlled by a remote in Damien's car, since he simply passed by the electronic keypad without stopping. Fin followed him through and, in the mirror, he saw the gates swinging closed again.

"What, no moat?" Suzy quipped.

"I'm more worried about Tyrannosaurs," Fin replied.

Once inside, amid scattered trees, a few buildings stood, constructed of the same rough-hewn stone. But the most prominent building was the house.

"Oh my god," Fin said, "his house is almost as weird as ours."

"At least his has a coherent design," Suzy replied, taking in the sight.

The house was a castle, very gothic and grim in grey granite, although as they got closer, Fin decided that it was actually constructed from textured cement blocks made to look like rough-hewn stone.

The road continued toward the castle and looped around into a circular drive in front of the main entry, which resembled the gates in the wall, but on a smaller scale.

High above the entry, a number of colorful pennants fluttered. They all flanked one flag in the center that, when the breeze opened it enough, Fin could see bore a logo, or rather a coat of arms, containing the word "Specter," which he had seen on TV advertisements of *King of the Dead*. Since Specter was not Damien's birth name, Fin assumed it was just a Medieval-styled logo that Damien had commissioned.

Damien pulled up to the door and Fin stopped behind him.

Lowering his voice to an ominous tone as Damien had in the coffee shop, Fin glanced at Suzy.

"Throwing caution to the wind," he said, "and oblivious to whatever ghastly horrors awaited them, the band of plucky ghost hunters threw themselves blindly into the haunted hustler's inner sanctum."

Suzy glanced back at him with what she thought was a sardonic grin. She attempted to roll her eyes, but her own misgivings about this case made it look less confident than she had hoped.

uite a place you've got here, Lustig," Fin said, looking around the courtyard as they all approached the front door.

"Lustig?" Damien echoed, frowning.

"Victor Lustig," Fin explained. "European con man. One of the most notorious con artists in history. He actually sold the Eiffel Tower twice. To my knowledge, though, he never tried to sell fake exorcisms."

Damien smiled and shook his head.

"You really think I'm any different than Harrison Ford or Brad Pitt? To an extent, yes, I'm an actor, a showman. I put on a show that people enjoy. What the hell's wrong with that?"

"Everybody knows *they're* acting," Suzy said. "You put yourself out there as a great spiritist, a ghost hunter, and that's what people believe."

Damien sighed.

"As I said, I *am* a ghost hunter, I *am* a spiritist. I do help people. All of that is real. But part of it is, admittedly, show-manship."

"Which your viewers buy as the real thing," Suzy insisted.

"We include a disclaimer in the credits on every single episode that the show is meant for entertainment purposes only."

"And we all know how absolutely everybody religiously reads all the credits," Fin said.

Damien shot him a grimace and cocked his head toward the door.

"Come inside. Let's get comfortable and talk."

He opened the door, a heavy oaken portal that looked perfectly at home in the pseudo-medieval castle. Suzy hoisted the baby carrier, then stopped.

"Before I take my baby inside there, I want to know for certain that it's safe."

"It's safe," Damien nodded. "The binding spell is doing what it's supposed to do."

"Then, how do you know this so-called evil spirit of yours is even still here?" Fin asked.

"I know," Damien replied gravely.

Fin and Suzy studied Damien's face, then they exchanged a look between themselves. They nodded and followed him inside.

The entry was actually pretty tasteful, a medieval motif, but nicely done, with wrought iron coat hooks. They paused here and hung their jackets on them. A stone-looking staircase rose up to the second floor on the left, but Damien led them past the staircase and through a door near the back.

Here, tastefulness met kitsch as they entered Damien's studio. The medieval motif continued but, here and there, Fin also recognized certain elements that reminded him of Frankenstein's laboratory from the original Boris Karloff movie. And from *Young Frankenstein*, since they used props from the original movie in that one, as well.

Over to the side was an easy chair with studio lights and two cameras aimed at it, with a small end table right next to it. Crosses and other grave markers were arranged as a backdrop behind the chair.

Even though Fin had never seen an episode of the show, he could imagine Damien sitting there, looking relaxed in the chair, the props of this room as a backdrop, as he wrapped up his shows. There were a couple of other chairs and a loveseat in the grouping, but the camera and lights were aimed at the one chair.

"Um, okay," Fin stammered, "this is kind of cool and, well, kind of weird."

Damien shrugged, but didn't bother to try to make a defense.

"Damien," Rachel said, her eyebrows bunched together, "have you ever considered the possibility of hallucinations?"

Damien turned to her and focused his attention on her. His piercing look almost made her shiver.

"What do you mean?" he asked.

"You have a brain tumor," she replied, her face implying that she was squeamish about mentioning it. "Is there any possibility that the evil spirit is simply a hallucination, a side effect of your illness?"

Damien smiled at her and shook his head. He reached his left hand over his head and pulled up the salt-and-pepper hair on the right and pulled down his collar with his right hand, revealing a long white scar snaking along the base of his skull.

"This is from a casserole dish that the demon threw at me. Left me with a concussion and twelve stitches. Seems pretty real to me."

"Yeah," Fin said, "I could show you a few scars of my own from when I totaled my Tesla a few years ago. That was because of hallucinations I was experiencing from a prescription drug. Our reactions may be real, and have very real consequences. Doesn't mean that what we're reacting *to* is real."

"The demon has been here for years. I was only diagnosed a few months ago."

"But couldn't hallucinations happen for a while before the cause is diagnosed?" Rachel asked.

"Probably," Damien conceded, "but likely not *several years* before." He smiled at Rachel, placing a hand on her shoulder. "I appreciate your attempts to normalize this, but I'm afraid there's nothing normal about it."

Suzy saw his hand stay on Rachel's shoulder, and do a couple of up and down caresses.

And she saw Rachel lean into his hand.

"Will we be able to meet your wife and daughter?" Suzy asked with an exaggeratedly innocent tone. Damien looked at her, but Suzy couldn't read the expression on his face.

"My wife is dead," he said, his tone somewhat addled.

Before Suzy could regain her composure, the conversation was interrupted by the sound of the door opening. They all turned to see who was entering.

Two girls stood there, one about ten or eleven years old, the other around sixteen.

"Claire said she thought she heard the gates," the older girl said.

"*You* didn't hear them?" Damien asked.

The older girl shrugged and smiled.

"I had my earbuds in."

Damien turned to his visitors.

"Fin, Suzy, Rachel," he motioned toward the new entries, "my girls, Shannon and Claire."

9

"ice to meet you," Fin said. Rachel did one better, by walking up to the girls to shake their hands. Suzy was feeling a little silly, having thought that Damien's references to 'his family' included a wife.

"Oh, you have a baby," Claire said with the imploring tone that little girls often use with babies and puppies, making a beeline toward Suzy. Suzy quickly recovered and smiled at the little blonde girl as she came to look at Julie. "Aw, she's so little! How old is she?"

"Just about seven months," Suzy said, her face breaking into an even larger smile as she took in the sight of her baby girl. Julie was asleep again, but with the sounds going on around her, it didn't seem to be very deep. Claire started to reach for her hand.

"Okay," Damien said, "Claire, honey, don't wake the baby."

Claire, unable to draw her eyes away from the baby, only nodded, but she pulled her hand away.

Suzy smiled at Claire. She wondered what Emma would have been like if she had lived to her age, just a couple more years. And she realized with a tug at her heart that Emma would nearly be the same age as Shannon if she were still alive.

"Shannon," Damien said, "why don't you and Claire go back to your rooms? We have some business to take care of, then I'll come up, and we'll talk about what to do for dinner. Okay?"

"Sure, Dad," Shannon replied, flicking her dark shoulder-length hair out of her face. She hadn't moved from the door since they had entered, though she did seem to be wavering between being an aloof teenager, and curious about the baby.

"Go on, honey," Damien said, guiding Claire back toward her big sister.

Suzy and Rachel both watched longingly after the girls. After Damien's daughters left, he directed his visitors over toward the seating area.

"Can I offer you anything to drink?" he asked.

From the choices he offered, Suzy and Rachel both took sparkling water, while Fin accepted a glass of 15-year-old Macallan single malt Scotch.

Damien sat down in the one chair that seemed to be his, the one that the lights and cameras were pointed at. Fin and Suzy sat on the loveseat, while Rachel sat down in one of the other chairs.

"So," Damien said, "those are my girls. They're the ones I am determined to protect."

"Damien," Suzy said contritely, "I'm sorry. I thought that, by saying 'my family,' you were including your wife. I didn't mean to be stupid."

"I'm afraid my wife died a few years ago, Suzy," Damien said quietly, without any blame in his voice.

His eyes expressed a hurt that still seemed fresh. He glanced back toward the door, as if to make sure that it was closed, and the girls were not still there to hear.

"Kate, my wife was not well," he said, his voice pitched a little quieter. "She suffered from severe depression." He took a pause and a deep breath. "Then, one day, she apparently decided that she'd had enough. She swallowed a bottle of sleeping pills and lay down on our bed for the last time."

Suzy and Fin glanced at each other, and Fin blew out a heavy sigh. He hoped it wasn't one of the girls who had found her.

"I'm so sorry, Damien," Rachel said, leaning toward him from her chair.

"Thank you," he replied quietly, as he covertly wiped away a tear that had escaped from his eye. "Do you—" he sighed, "do you have any idea how hard it is being a spiritist, yet not being able to make contact with the love of your life?"

"Yes," Suzy replied quietly, "I do."

Fin looked at her. It had long been a difficult thing for him, knowing that she lost her husband while she was still in love with him. He thought that it would have been much easier—for himself, at least—if they had simply fallen out of love and gotten divorced.

But Fin knew that Suzy loved him. Whether he was the "love of her life" or not, he still struggled with that, when he dared to think about it.

"Who's going to take care of your daughters when you're gone?" Suzy asked. From the corner of her eye, Suzy saw Rachel look at her, and she knew what was on her mind.

Damien smiled.

"James, my cameraman, is their godfather. He's agreed to take them."

"I would have thought," Rachel said, "that you would have chosen Terry, since he's always so concerned about safety."

There was a slight quirk around her lips that Suzy recognized when her best friend was making a subtle joke, though never having seen the show, Suzy didn't get it. The men didn't seem to notice.

"That—well, that's actually an act," Damien replied, with an apprehensive glance at Suzy. He looked back at Rachel, even leaning toward her as he spoke. "He's the nervous and panicky 'voice of reason' in the face of James and me bravely rushing headlong into the fray."

He looked down for a moment, thoughtful.

"But I've known James for years. He knew all about Kate's depression—my wife." He glanced at Fin and Suzy, then back to Rachel. "James is the one who helped me get through Kate's suicide. He's a good man, and both of the girls love him."

"What do your daughters think about what you plan to do?" Suzy asked wearing a troubled frown. Damien looked at her.

"Claire doesn't know anything about it, but I have confided in Shannon." He paused for a few moments. "I mean, Claire does know that I'm dying, but she doesn't know that I'm planning on bringing the curtain down myself."

He paused for a deep breath.

"Given Shannon's disbelief in the supernatural, she's a little less than enthusiastic about what I'm planning on doing. But she knows that I'm already dying, and that I'm not just planning on killing myself for no reason, like her mother did."

"It wasn't for no reason," Fin said. "If she was seriously depressed, well, that was the reason. Too many people just don't realize how real and uncontrollable and overpowering depression can be."

"Of course," Damien replied, nodding and waving a hand as if he had heard it before. "But, well, you know what I mean." He pressed his lips together for a moment. "There was nothing tangible that I could point to, for my girls, at their age, to make them understand why their mother had killed herself."

The others looked at him with varying expressions of sympathy.

Damien took a deep, fortifying breath. He squinted, massaging the side of his head as if he had a headache. He took a sip from his glass and sighed, closing his eyes for a moment.

"Anyway, I had hoped not to go there." He looked at his visitors. "So, what do you think about my idea for the show?"

"I still think it's insane," Suzy said without a moment's hesitation, but then, with a glance toward the door, she softened her tone, "but I think I can understand it a lot more now."

"So, you'll do it?" Damien asked, expressing more hope than he had since they had met.

"She didn't say that," Fin replied quickly. He glanced at Suzy, pausing thoughtfully. "This is still something way beyond our experience. We're going to have to do some research and some consulting and give it some serious thought before we agree to this."

Suzy nodded her agreement. Damien looked at both of them, and he nodded back, giving a grateful smile.

10

Dinner was served in a dining room that reminded Fin of a small banquet hall from *Game of Thrones*. The walls were sections of exposed stone interspersed with massive oak timbers. The ceiling boasted dark, heavy timbers, as well, and was lit by candle chandeliers. He thought they seemed to be electrical versions, but very good facsimiles.

Damien had asked if they were planning on driving back home that evening. When Fin replied that they would get a hotel for the night and go back in the morning, Damien insisted they stay at his home.

Daryna, the fortyish Ukrainian *au pair* that Damien employed to keep house and care for his girls, had prepared a delicious meal. Damien was not there to enjoy it, though. His headache had worsened, and he had excused himself for the evening.

"Daryna," Fin asked, "how long have you worked for Damien?"

"Mr. Specter hired me just after wife died," she replied. Fin thought her accent sounded like Russian, though a little softer, not quite as harsh. Her face suddenly looked very distraught. "He was so sad," she added, "and did not think he could care for daughters by himself."

Fin nodded sympathetically.

"He called her the love of his life," he said.

Daryna nodded.

"He love her so much," she replied, tears pooling in her eyes. She started to say more but sighed and shook her head sadly.

Rachel looked at the girls and saw sadness on their faces, as well.

"What do you think of your dad's show?" she asked Claire, hoping to raise the mood at the table. The little girl's face instantly expressed a level of excitement easily accessed by children of her age.

"I think it's so much fun!" she enthused, her eyes wide. "Daddy lets me watch some of them." Her face implied, though, that she wished she could see more than just *some*. "He gets to talk to dead people and help them go to heaven."

Shannon's face wore a bit of a smirk at Claire's response, her dark eyebrows shading her blue eyes, the same color as Damien's, but Rachel didn't want to spoil Claire's perception of the show by asking her opinion.

She was happy to see that Shannon, apparently, didn't want to spoil it, either. She kept her obvious thoughts to herself and smiled at Claire when the little girl cast an excited look at her. Rachel got the impression that Shannon had already assumed an almost motherly position over her little sister.

Then, Claire's face changed again.

"Daddy's going to heaven, too," she said as the sadness returned. "He's dying." Tears welled up on her eyelids, then broke free, rolling down her cheeks.

"I know, honey," Rachel replied. "I'm so sorry."

Before the words were even out of her mouth, Shannon was on her knees next to Claire's chair, comforting her little sister.

Rachel sighed and looked at Suzy and Fin, her lips quirked in a helpless frown.

» § «

"Well," Suzy said as they entered their room and Fin closed the door, "that was —"

"Awkward?" Fin finished, nodding.

"I was thinking agonizing, but awkward works, too, if you're going for understatement."

"Most people become orphans eventually," Fin said, "but it sucks when it happens that early in life."

Claire had been nearly inconsolable. With Shannon's attempts to soothe her, she began to calm down. But Daryna came to the other side of Claire's chair to assist and, still emotional about Damien having lost the love of his life years before, had the little girl crying again in no time.

"Poor Rachel," Suzy said.

"I know," Fin agreed, placing their suitcase and Julie's carrier on the bed, while Suzy divested herself of the diaper bag.

Though Suzy had fed her some baby food during dinner, she was fussy, and Suzy was glad. She sat herself down in a massive oaken chair that was still comfortable, she was surprised to find, thanks to the cushions and throw pillows on it. She pulled up her blouse and unhooked the cup on her bra, while Fin carried the baby to her. When Julie started nursing, Suzy audibly sighed.

"You never make that sound when *I* do that," Fin quipped.

"If I'm engorged and Julie's asleep," Suzy said, "you're welcome to have a go at it."

Fin smiled and left Suzy and Julie to do their symbiotic thing. Suzy was looking down at Julie, while the baby was sharply focused on Suzy, looking at her intently. The baby reached up to Suzy's face, her fingers reaching, but ultimately grasping air. Suzy smiled at her and offered a finger to hold onto.

Fin found a place to put their suitcase, then pulled down the covers on the bed.

"So," he said, "what are your thoughts about this case now?"

Suzy was quiet for a while, and the only sound in the room was the gentle rhythm of Julie nursing. Fin was pondering whether to repeat the question or to just wait, when Suzy responded.

"I feel a lot more open to it, now," she replied. "And I'm very sure a lot of that has to do with getting to know the girls a little."

Fin nodded as he sat down on the edge of the bed, a troubled expression on his face. He looked down at his feet, thoughtful about the case, and about Suzy's more positive response.

"Still doesn't change the fact that I know nothing about evil spirits," Suzy continued, "or if there's even such a thing as demons."

Fin raised his eyebrows and nodded his head a little more vigorously as she expressed his own concerns, which he readily admitted went back to his earlier life.

"I'll definitely have to pay a visit to Lilith."

Fin looked up at her.

"But," he replied, "I thought you said several months ago that you had outpaced Lilith's knowledge and experience. 'The grasshopper has surpassed the master,' I believe were your exact words."

"About ghosts," Suzy nodded, "yes, that's what she said. I've never had anything to do with demons, though. I don't know if Lilith has, either, but she's definitely where I need to start."

"So," Fin said guardedly, looking across at her, "I haven't sensed any kind of ghostly presence since we've been here. Have you?"

"I'm not sure."

Having relieved some of the pressure, Suzy deftly rotated Julie and placed the baby on her other breast. After locking eyes with Julie for a few moments, she looked up at Fin.

"There's something here, but I can't really place it."

Fin frowned.

"You know that feeling that someone's watching you?" Suzy asked. Fin nodded. "It's kind of like that. It's like somebody's there, and you feel the hair on the back of your neck rise. I know there's somebody here, but I can't see them or make contact."

Fin sighed, not feeling any better having heard her response.

» § «

Rachel looked around her bedchamber. Upon walking in to it, she had decided immediately that the word "bedroom" was just a little too generic and common, and that "bedchamber" seemed more apropos. This really did look like a bedchamber in a Medieval castle, from the carved wood panels on the walls and the heavily timbered ceiling, to the rich draperies hung beside the windows and the tapestries on the walls.

Then, there was the bed, a beautiful thing with heavy covers and ornately carved oak posts that supported an equally ornately carved tester, with more gorgeous drapes and sheers at the head.

There were two windows, generously sized, set deeply into the wood and stone walls, one on each side of the bed. She realized that they were likely more than would have graced the bedchamber of a real castle in the Middle Ages, and the light they shed on the room, even in the evening, was likely more than genuine Medieval denizens of such a structure would have enjoyed in their time. Still, the "candle" chandelier, lit by a switch on the wall, cast a warm glow over the interior.

Leaving her suitcase beside the door, she went to the bed and sat down. She practically purred as she felt a modern luxurious mattress supporting several layers of soft, warm covers, topped by a beautiful old-styled silk damask comforter.

As soon as she sat, she felt the fatigue wash over her. At first, she couldn't understand it. She had done little more than sit all day—in Fin's car, in the coffee shop, and here in Damien's house. But then she remembered that sitting in a car for a road trip, even a short one, can cause muscle tension, lethargy and sluggish blood circulation.

Besides that, she realized that she had also experienced some heightened emotions, as well.

Learning that Damien was dying was a big one, which initially struck her as odd, considering that she didn't even know him. But then, she remembered feeling particularly sad and depressed when Alan Rickman had died several years before, and a few other celebrities, people she had never met, but had gotten to know through their roles, their music, or their public personas.

Damien, she had come to know through his show, and now, she had also actually met and conversed with him. She *did* know him.

But even more than Damien, Rachel recognized that the bulk of her melancholy was due to Shannon and Claire. Such precious girls, they had already lost their mother, and soon they would lose their father.

She thought of their sweet faces, their ready smiles, and her heart broke for them.

11

The dark drama of the night before had vanished by the time Rachel got downstairs the next morning. She had apologies ready, but when she saw Damien joking around with the girls, she decided it would be better to not even mention the previous evening.

"Hi, Rachel," Damien smiled as she came into the dining room.

"Good morning," she said, feeling that curious flutter in her stomach that she had felt the day before. "How are you feeling?"

"Better," he nodded, "thank you. These two help." He poked both girls in the belly. Claire giggled and hunched over, grasping the spot that his finger had poked. Shannon simply rolled her eyes, but she still had a ready smile for Rachel.

A faint beeping noise sounded from some other room, and Rachel frowned, trying to identify the sound. Damien saw her puzzled look and identified it for her.

"That's telling us the gate is opening. I invited Terry and James over for breakfast so that Suzy and Fin can meet them."

"The whole crew!" Rachel replied with a smile. "How fun!"

Moments later, Suzy and Fin entered the medieval banquet hall at the same time that Daryna led the two men into the room. Julie was awake and cradled in Suzy's arm, though Suzy carried the empty carrier in her other hand. The baby was looking around intently at the people and the strange surroundings.

"Uncle James!" Claire shouted as she ran into James' arms.

"I know," he gushed enthusiastically, wrapping his arms around her with a big smile on his face, "it's almost like you haven't seen me since the day before yesterday!" Rachel smiled seeing how much both of the girls seemed to love James.

Introductions were made, and Rachel was admittedly more excited than the others to meet the supporting cast of *King of the Dead*.

James and Claire cooed over the baby, which Julie loved, while Daryna placed plates of omelets on the table. Rachel noticed that she only set six places. After the dishes were served, Daryna directed the girls out of the room.

"Come, *moyi myli divchata*," she said, "and we will leave grownups to talk their business."

The grownups settled in their places around the table, as Julie gazed fixedly up at Suzy from her carrier. Suzy kept stealing glances back at her, making faces and smiling, causing the baby to smile back at her and kick her feet up and down excitedly.

After everyone had begun digging into their breakfast, Damien cleared his throat.

"So," he said in a 'get down to business' voice, and he looked at Suzy, "I invited James and Terry here so that you and Fin could meet them, kind of get a feel for the show, since you've never actually seen an episode of it." He raised an eyebrow as he looked toward his crew.

Terry uttered a melodramatic gasp, which got a laugh from the others.

"*I* watch your show," Rachel said with a mock recalcitrant tone. She glanced at Suzy with her own eyebrows raised. "I'm sorry, Suzy, but I'm just feeling the need to distance myself from you two." Suzy smiled at her, and a few chuckles were heard around the table.

"If *you* had a show," James said, looking at Suzy and Fin, "I'd definitely watch it. I've been hearing about you guys for a while."

"Really?" Fin asked.

"Of course, not on the 'legitimate' news." He made air quotes. "But a couple of the more reputable paranormal websites have published bits and pieces about you over the last few years."

"Wait," Terry said, putting his fork down, his eyes expanding, "these are the ones you told me about a while ago?"

Fin and Suzy looked at Terry, their eyebrows drawn together curiously.

"They are," James nodded.

Terry dramatically sat back in his chair and turned to Suzy, his eyes wide.

"You actually crossed the veil and confronted a ghost in the spirit world, on his own turf?"

"Ah," Suzy said, "sure, I guess that one did get a little national coverage a few years back."

"It helped that it was actually witnessed by two doctors, a nurse and a physician's assistant," Fin said.

"God, that's so cool!" Terry enthused. "So? What was it like?"

He was still looking at Fin, so Fin shook his head.

"I'm afraid I didn't see it. I was comatose."

"Oh, that's right," Terry said, "you were the one in the hospital bed." Fin nodded.

"What luck," Damien said, "being sent to a haunted hospital."

"Yeah, I didn't feel so lucky at the time."

Suzy was feeling uncomfortable with herself and Fin being the center of attention. She realized she hadn't learned anything about Damien's team, and she hoped to change the subject.

"So, what do you do?" she asked, looking back and forth at Terry and James.

"I'm the cameraman," James said. "What I do, usually, is struggle to make these two goons look good."

Terry picked up his fork with a flourish that somehow left his middle finger pointing up toward James.

"I'm the tech guy," he said. "I handle the EMF meters and the EVP recorders, and all that fun stuff."

He took a bite of his omelet and looked up at Fin.

"What kind of equipment do you guys use?" he asked, the words muffled around the food in his mouth.

"No equipment," Fin said, shaking his head. "We connect directly with the spirit, mind-to-mind."

"Oh my god," Terry enthused, his eyes wide again, "that's so meta!" He turned his attention to Damien. "Boss, I think these guys are on a whole different fucking level from us."

"Yeah, I already know that," Damien nodded wearing a sage expression. He looked up at his men, and he sighed. "They're the real thing." He saw Terry's eyebrows lower a little, and he nodded again. "Yes, they know that we, shall we say, embellish a lot of our cases. Or, at least, the effects."

James and Terry both looked at Suzy and Fin with an expression that could only be described as embarrassment. With all attention focused on her and Fin yet again, Suzy asked another question.

"So, what do you guys think about Damien's grand design?"

"Huh?" Terry asked.

"His plan to kill himself on national television. Surely, he's told you."

James and Terry's faces changed instantly at the reminder of Damien's upcoming demise.

"I think it's a good plan," James finally replied somberly. "Obviously, it's not the outcome any of us want, but given the circumstances, I think it covers all the bases, assuming that evil spirit can be sent away."

"Have either of you seen or heard or otherwise experienced this spirit?" Fin asked.

"No," Terry answered immediately.

James leaned forward and pondered a moment before answering.

"Not for several years," he said. He glanced at Terry, then back at Suzy and Fin. "I've known Damien for a long time. Years ago, I felt some weird shit here. But I'm no spiritist, so I can't really tell you anything about it."

"Just tell us what it was like," Suzy nudged. "What did you see?"

"I didn't *see* anything. I didn't *hear* anything." He shook his head apologetically. "Whenever I was around, it was always after the fact. Damien would tell me about something crazy that had just happened, but I never actually saw it happen."

"So," Fin frowned, "it's just hearsay, then. You just took Damien's word for it?" Fin looked across at their host. "Sorry, Damien."

Damien just smiled lightly and shrugged, motioning for James to continue. James pulled his eyebrows together and shook his head.

"No, there was always something there. Even though I never witnessed the occurrence, I could always feel — something. You know that sensation you get that someone's watching you?"

Suzy looked at Fin, recalling her similar expression the night before.

"Yeah," she nodded. "I've been feeling that since we've been here."

James looked at her, a look of amazement on his face.

"Damn, you really *are* the real deal," he said. "I haven't felt that since Damien put the binding spell on the spirit."

12

I don't know," Suzy said regretfully. She closed her eyes and sighed. "What I said yesterday still stands. We just don't have any experience in this."

"But," Damien replied, "you said you'll check with your advisor, right?"

Suzy looked at him, wishing she hadn't mentioned Lilith at breakfast.

"I will," she nodded, "but like I said, I have no idea if she has any experience with demons, either."

Fin came back in, having loaded the last of their luggage into his car. Suzy looked back at Damien.

"I'll definitely let you know. I'm afraid that's the best I can tell you for now."

"That's all I ask," Damien smiled. "I appreciate anything you can do."

Suzy glanced at Rachel who was looking sympathetically at Damien. Terry and James stood quietly, a little in the background, not wanting to impinge on Damien's space or request.

"Damien," Fin said, sticking his hand out, "thank you for your hospitality. And however our part in this turns out," he glanced at Suzy, "I wish you all the best."

"Thank you, Fin," Damien said with a sincere smile, shaking his hand firmly.

"I do, too," Suzy said, holding her hand out. Damien took it and enclosed it in both of his.

"I appreciate that, Suzy." He pulled his left hand away and reached for his back pocket. Before he let go of her hand, he slipped a business card into it. "Just in case you forget my number."

"Oh, I've got your number, alright," she said with her signature smartass grin. "But thank you."

Damien turned toward Rachel.

"Rachel, it was truly a pleasure to meet and get to know you."

He started to reach his hand out toward her, but she went in for a hug. Damien sighed and smiled, wrapping his arms around her.

Rachel let go of him and backed away, glancing at the others in the entryway.

"Sorry," she said, a little embarrassed.

"I'm not," Damien replied, placing a hand on her shoulder. Despite what Suzy was inclined to think of him, she was impressed that his response sounded sincere without being slimy.

Terry and James were pulled into the group as the goodbyes were being said. Then, Suzy picked up Julie's carrier, and she, Fin and Rachel went outside. The three men watched from the door as Fin and Rachel settled in their seats, and Suzy buckled the baby into the car.

"So, Ron," James said, "what'll you do if she decides she can't help you?"

Damien shook his head as he watched Suzy get in the car and fasten her seatbelt.

"I can't think about that now."

» § «

"King of the Dead?" Fin snickered. "Really? The guy's all show biz and little else."

Suzy sighed and nodded, looking down at the business card in her hand. She was inclined to agree with Fin, but she was not quite sure of her overall assessment of the self-professed King of the Dead.

"The man's dying!" Rachel shot from the back seat. "Can't you be a little more sympathetic to his situation, if nothing else?"

Suzy and Fin caught their breath at the sudden outburst behind them.

"Sorry," Fin said contritely.

"Sure, honey," Suzy said, turning back to look at her friend. Rachel's face revealed the empathy she felt toward Damien, and the sadness she felt over his situation. Suzy quirked her lips into a regretful smile. "I'm sorry. I know we tend to be smartasses but, well, you do know that we, at least, try to be good and decent people."

Rachel nodded.

"I know," she said. "I'm sorry, too. I just—I know how you both feel about him, and I respect that. But it's just so sad." She sighed. "Those poor sweet girls," she finished, with tears suddenly filling her eyes.

Tears abruptly filled Suzy's eyes, as well. She had experienced a similar feeling toward Damien's daughters, and felt sad over their hopeless situation. And she felt regretful about Rachel's feelings.

"Sweetie, I promise, if I think there's anything I can do to help him, I definitely will."

13

This is some weird shit," Fin said. "Or it would be if we hadn't witnessed very similar things ourselves." Then, he looked off to the side, as if reconsidering. "Okay, it's still weird, but not unheard of."

Back home in Marblehead, Suzy had come into Fin's study at the top of the corner turret, to check in and see what he was up to. She was holding and petting their Pomeranian, Ursula, whom she had just picked up from their neighbors, Terri and Art.

The little dog, at sight of Fin, began wiggling excitedly in Suzy's arms.

"What are you talking about?" Suzy asked.

Fin looked at Ursula for a moment and smiled. He reached out and gave the dog a distracted scratch behind the ears and under her collar. Then, he looked back down at his computer.

"I'm reading about some historical reports of so-called demon possession," he replied, getting serious again. "This one is the case that inspired William Peter Blatty to write *The Exorcist*. Roland Doe — which was a pseudonym …" Fin squinted at the screen, then nodded, "Ronald Edwin Hunkeler, a 14-year-old boy in Maryland, was being harassed by an evil spirit. Furniture and dishes would move of their own volition, the boy's bed would shake violently, and words would spontaneously appear scratched into his body."

Suzy shuddered and unconsciously grasped her wrist, remembering bloody letters being sliced into it by an unseen ghostly straight razor just a few months earlier. Ursula looked up at her a little alarmed at her sudden tension. Suzy powered through the feeling. She put Ursula down, and the dog, after a few turns, settled in the bed that Fin had placed there for her.

"No projectile vomiting, though?" Suzy had never seen the movie, but she knew how much of a cultural phenomenon Linda Blair's pea-green vomit had become.

"No, although that was mentioned in an earlier exorcism, in 1928," Fin replied. He scrolled a little on the computer. "Then, there's Gina."

"Gina who?"

"Just Gina. No last name was given. This was the most-watched episode in the history of the news show *20/20*. In 1991, this 16-year-old girl was suffering from psychotic episodes. Two priests were engaged to exorcise the spirit that was supposedly possessing her, and *20/20* was there to record it.

"According to one of the priests, she would have levitated to the ceiling if she hadn't been tied down to the bed. During the six-hour exorcism, she thrashed against the restraints, growled and cursed at the priests, and spoke in tongues.

"The priests claimed that they cast out two demons, named Zion and Minga, after which Gina felt better.

"Of course, not long after this episode, the girl was hospitalized again with similar symptoms, and this time, she was treated with antipsychotic drugs instead of holy water and Latin."

"So," Suzy said, looking at him through narrowed eyelids, "it seems to me that it's your belief that it's all just bullshit?"

Fin peered at the computer screen for a few moments before drawing his gaze away to look at Suzy.

"I don't know," he finally said. "Based on the beliefs in my previous life with the religious zealots, demon possession is a very real thing, although they would certainly never endorse Catholic priests reciting incantations and sprinkling holy water." He drew in a deep breath and slowly blew it out. "I don't really see *you* going the holy water route, either."

"Nor do I," Suzy replied. "But since it's my first exorcism, I think I'm going to have to rely on guidance from more experienced sources."

» § «

Rachel hadn't gone upstairs to her bedroom, yet. After the last couple of days, she just felt emotionally drained. In the Sunday evening traffic, the drive back to her home in Boston from Suzy's house in Marblehead had taken nearly an hour, adding to her fatigue. She had dropped her suitcase at the foot of the stairs and just meandered around her house.

Her home was decorated in an early American motif, with lots of tchotchkes and knick-knacks, as Suzy called them, mostly from the colonial era. She had collections of pewter dishes and mugs, several silver pieces, including some actually cast by Paul Revere. She had several framed portraits — alas, all prints — of several of the Founding Fathers. There were early American-style quilts draped here and there on her furniture, though she had one on prominent display in a glass case. This one, which she had paid handsomely for, had been made by Betsy Ross in her pre-flag-making upholstering days.

Immersing herself in all the elements of her home had always had a calming effect on Rachel, but now, she realized that she actually felt a little more tense. She stopped where she was and looked around, trying to figure out the source of that feeling.

She was standing in front of an antique hutch and buffet which contained numerous decorative plates with early American flag designs. She noticed dust and cobwebs on them, which reminded her of Suzy's remarks, on a number of occasions, that all of these dust-catchers would be too much for her friend to stay on top of.

Rachel knew it was time to do some house-cleaning, and in her current state, it just felt like too much. Rachel had always been a high-energy person, which had, several times, teased out a smartass comment from Suzy about making her tired.

The way she felt now, Rachel could definitely understand that.

For the first time in years, she started considering the possibility of a home makeover. Maybe it was time to chuck the tchotchkes, to take on a more easily manageable design scheme.

It was a jarring thought, but she allowed it to linger. More than jarring, it was almost disorienting. This had been her style, her identity, personal individuality, for more years than she could even remember. To actually be considering changing it felt bewildering to her.

But she recognized that she was getting older. She had noticed a number of times in recent memory when she had wished things were easier, a little less complicated. Maybe this was another example of that wish.

Her short time with Jeff, Fin's friend and Best Man from Colorado, came to mind. He had stayed for several days after the wedding, after Suzy and Fin had left for their honeymoon in Colorado, and they had grown close. He had paid several visits to her in her home, and he had made similar comments about how "busy" her décor was. She couldn't disagree with him.

Their relationship, if it was enough to be called that, had continued for a while after he returned home, but she had called it quits almost a year back. While she wasn't necessarily missing Jeff, she was missing that closeness. This current fatigue she was feeling, added to the realization of her aloneness, felt like a burden, a weight that she could scarcely bear.

It was an almost crushing thought, when she realized that she was lonely. She had always been an easygoing woman, a textbook happy-go-lucky person. Now, Rachel recognized that all her friends were married or in relationships, while she still lived alone in her cluttered, dust-catching house.

She was enough of a feminist to know that she didn't need a man to be complete. But she was lonely enough to know that she *wanted* a man to not feel so desolate and solitary.

From there, her thoughts drifted to Damien, and his fast-approaching end of life. She thought of Claire and Shannon, and she wiped away a tear.

The fatigue was sitting heavy on her shoulders, and she decided that it was time to settle in for the night. To carry her suitcase upstairs, to put her things away, and get ready for bed.

Alone.

14

Suzy was surprised when Lilith opened the door. Her diminutive advisor on all things ghostly had always seemed old to her yet, Suzy realized, a little mystified, strangely ageless. But Lilith looked particularly haggard this morning.

She was also leaning on a walker.

"Lilith," Suzy said sympathetically as she came into the house, "what happened?"

Lilith shook her head and sighed as she closed the door.

"It was really stupid of me," she said self-deprecatingly. "I got old."

Suzy did a double take at her response.

"Hey, are you becoming a smartass?"

"I guess you're rubbing off on me," Lilith replied with a tired grin. "Come on in."

They went into Lilith's living room, its perimeters lined, as always, with crystals of various shapes, sizes and colors. On several horizontal spaces were candles, some of which were burning and, combined with the scent of incense, gave the room the cozy smell of a gift shop. Not quite overpowering, Suzy found it comforting, and she settled easily into her usual chair.

"I was surprised to hear from you," Lilith said as she eased herself into her chair. Usually, her feet dangled an inch or two above the floor, but this time, she didn't go to the trouble to push herself back on the seat. She just sat near the front of the cushion and leaned back in a somewhat slouchy posture. "I'm afraid my level of experience hasn't changed, while I suspect yours has risen even since we talked last."

"You're still my friend," Suzy replied, wondering momentarily if she should offer to help push her back on the chair.

"That's true," Lilith smiled. "And it's always a pleasure to see you."

"Which," Suzy sighed, "makes me feel embarrassed to say that I actually do have something of a spiritual nature to ask you about."

Lilith looked confused.

"But as I said, you've gone beyond my level of experience. I don't feel like I can advise you any further."

"About ghosts," Suzy replied. "I'm not here about ghosts. I don't think."

The confusion turned to intrigue as Lilith placed her hands on the seat cushion and pushed herself into a more upright position.

"I'm listening," she said quietly.

"What do you know about evil spirits?" Suzy asked with some trepidation. Lilith's eyebrows went up.

"Not a lot, I'm afraid. I know bits and pieces of historical information and beliefs, but I don't have much first-hand experience."

"Anything you can tell me would be greatly appreciated."

"First of all," Lilith started in a cautious voice, "I don't like to call them evil spirits. They exist, it's true, but it's not our place to judge them as evil."

"So, you're saying they're not dangerous?"

"Oh, no, I'm not saying that at all." Lilith lowered her eyebrows and thought for a moment. She looked up at Suzy. "Do you think lions are evil?"

"No, of course not," Suzy replied.

"A zebra might disagree with you," Lilith nodded. "From the zebra's point of view, lions are evil creatures. A beast that preys on them, kills them, slices their bellies open and eats them. But to a lion, a zebra is just food."

"Huh," Suzy said. "Okay, just for conversational purposes, what should we call them?"

"I prefer daemon. It's from early Greek."

"Okay," Suzy agreed. "Sounds a lot like demon, but if that's what you prefer, that's what I'll call them."

"That is, in fact, where the word demon comes from. But in its original form, it wasn't considered necessarily evil."

"Fin says that, in his previous life, demons were angels that rebelled against God and joined Satan in an effort to deceive and draw away humans."

"That is, certainly, one viewpoint," Lilith agreed. She cocked her head to the side. "Did you know that I'm named after a demon?"

"What?" Suzy asked, shocked. "I had no idea."

"To be fair, I doubt that my parents had any idea, either, about that, but according to early Mesopotamian and Jewish mythology, Lilith was the first wife of Adam, before the story of creation in Genesis. According to the stories, particularly in the Talmud of Babylon, Lilith was banished from the Garden of Eden for not being obedient and submissive to Adam. She is now considered a primordial she-demon."

"Damn! You were a born feminist!" Suzy said.

"Yes," Lilith nodded with a humble smile. "Her name is even found in the Bible, though not giving reference to who she was in the ancient stories. In Isaiah 34:14, the word 'lilit' is given, but in most versions is translated as 'night creature.'"

"Okay," Suzy said, "this is interesting, but Fin is no longer religious. I'm not either, and I'm hoping I won't have to set up an account with the Catholic Church to purchase a jug of holy water. What else can you tell me?"

"Well," Lilith replied, her eyes darting back and forth as she recalled the bits and pieces, "stories about daemons, divine ones, spiritual entities, are as varied as they are ancient. Virtually every known civilization has had folklore about some such supernatural creature."

"Can they be removed without employing a priest?" Suzy asked.

"Do you have a daemon?" Lilith asked cautiously.

"I don't, but somebody is wanting me to help them get rid of one."

"*Help* them?"

"Yes, well, he has some experience, though, like me, no specific experience with demons. It's Damien Specter, the *King of the Dead* guy."

Lilith rolled her eyes.

"Pssshh," she scoffed.

"I know," Suzy agreed. "We met him yesterday. Fin and I both agree that he's a little ridiculous, and pretty full of himself. But," she paused thoughtfully, "there are some persuasive reasons for us to be considering helping him with this."

Suzy leaned forward, her elbows on her knees.

"So, you said you don't believe they're evil."

"I said I don't believe it's our place to *judge* them as evil. They can be dangerous and predatory, but that's just their nature, like a lion. I think of a person who is evil as someone who's profoundly wicked and immoral, someone who has a sense of right and wrong, and who chooses to do the wrong thing, even if, or maybe *especially* if it harms someone else.

"Whether that's the case with daemons or not, I don't know. And it might vary from one to another.

"But, again, even if this one is not inherently evil, having a different motivation doesn't make it any less dangerous to us. We still need to take precautions."

"Okay," Suzy nodded, "what kind of precautions?"

"Well, like I said, I have little personal experience. But I understand that some people have had success with spells found in old grimoires." Lilith looked obliquely at her. "But you're probably too sensible, and think that's a little too silly and impractical."

"Huh," Suzy sneered. "Lilith, the last few years, I've learned not to be too quick to judge 'impractical' stuff like that."

"Well," Lilith replied, "with grimoires, belief is important. Belief puts more power behind your actions. If you have any doubts, any doubts at all, it may be better to have the spell performed by someone who believes.

"And many believers insist that magic spells can be strengthened by blood."

"Blood?" Suzy asked, an ominous tone in her voice. "We need to offer up a sacrifice?"

"No," Lilith smiled, "just a few drops are usually sufficient. Whoever is performing the ritual can just prick their thumb and allow the blood to drip while reciting the incantation.

"Also, the older the better. The ancients were more closely connected to the spirit world, so the ancient wisdom is often more effective."

"Damien has what he called an ancient grimoire," Suzy mused. "He used a binding spell from it to render the demon safe for his family."

"Perhaps you should check with him to see if there's a spell in his grimoire for expelling a daemon," Lilith suggested. She drew her eyebrows together. "If there is, I wonder why he didn't use it, instead of just a binding spell."

"I don't think he knows much about it himself," Suzy nodded. "I'll check with him, though. Thank you."

It had been a long day. Rachel usually enjoyed her job in the State Treasurer's office, in the gold-domed State House in Boston, but today, her heart and mind just weren't in it. Most days, she felt comfortable with the "red tape" that most people abhorred. She was familiar enough with it that she was able to help people "cut through it," which made her job satisfying and rewarding.

Today, she had been annoyed almost her entire time there.

Whenever she had a moment to examine her feelings, she realized that Damien Specter, and particularly 'his girls,' Claire and Shannon, were the cause of her irritability. Their plight weighed heavily on her mind, and she frequently found herself wiping tears from her eyes, often with some irritation.

She found herself in need of comfort.

At 4:30, she dug her cell phone out of her purse and pulled up Steve's number. Steve Monroe lived in a brick townhome on Marlborough Street, just a few blocks away in Beacon Hill. She listened to the phone ringing his number, but there was no answer.

She didn't leave a message.

She had met Steve several years before. Mark and Emma, Suzy's husband and daughter, had just died, and Rachel had made a point of spending as much time with Suzy as she could. She knew that Suzy's grief and loneliness would be overwhelming, and she didn't want her friend to go through it alone.

In time, though, Suzy insisted that she needed some time to herself. Rachel was familiar with Suzy's somewhat dark

sense of humor, but she didn't know how that would trans-
late to a truly dark and humorless real-life situation. But
when Suzy demanded it, Rachel acquiesced. She backed off,
though she had contacted a couple of other friends to keep
tabs on Suzy when Rachel wasn't with her.

Not knowing what to do with herself as she left work that
day, she ended up in a Dunkin' Donuts near the State
House. As she sat at a table with her head resting in her
hands, she heard a sympathetic voice.

"Are you okay?"

Rachel looked up and saw him. The man was in his forties, well-dressed without being ostentatious, a twinkle in
his eye and gleaming blond hair. He seemed sincerely concerned about her.

"I'm fine," she said, in a voice that was not convincing in
the least. The man sat down.

"I don't believe you," he said. Rachel smiled, not because
it was funny, but because she felt the relief of some of the
burden being shifted to someone else's shoulders.

She spent nearly a half hour telling Steve about Suzy and
about the death of her husband and daughter. Steve really
was sympathetic, and she felt herself drawn to him. It
wasn't a matter of attraction, not in the sense of what usually attracted her to a man. But he was real. His sympathy
was sincere.

She spent the night with him.

They didn't have sex, but he had held her, comforting
her, holding her in his arms as she slept. It had been just
what she had needed.

A few weeks later, Steve had called Rachel, feeling sad
after a woman he had been seeing every now and then had
broken up with him. Rachel had gone to him after work, and
they had a nice dinner together.

When they went to bed, it had been much like the last
time, except that Rachel was the one doing the comforting.
They both woke up in the middle of the night, and they

opened up more to each other. The lovemaking had been sweet and reciprocal.

From that night on, they called on each other when one of them needed comfort or closeness. They had helped each other through difficult times—breakups, Rachel's difficulty with a coworker, Steve's mother dying, or when one—or both—of them were lonely.

Their relationship had grown organically. Neither of them had forced it, nor had they tried to make it more than it was. They were not in love, but they were more than just friends. It was what many people referred to as a "friends with benefits" situation, though Rachel had always thought that label seemed trite.

From that first time, their lovemaking had always been tender and caring, and they helped each other through numerous tragedies. Steve became Rachel's personal relief valve, and vice versa. When Rachel felt particularly lonely, when she needed to feel someone in her arms, when she needed to feel a man inside her, Steve was the one she called.

Then, Jeff came along when Suzy and Fin got married. He had filled a void in her life, and he had suffused her with happiness. But it had been only temporary.

When Rachel broke up with him, Suzy was going through some hormonal difficulties related to her pregnancy, and with a ghost, and with Fin, and Rachel was there for her. Her best friend, and the birth of Julie, served as a diversion for Rachel. She had gotten through her breakup with Jeff without calling Steve.

Now, though, Suzy and Fin were busy with their baby, and they were puzzling through whether or not they should help Damien—and Claire and Shannon, she couldn't help adding. Rachel didn't want to burden them, or influence their decision, with her feelings.

Steve was the logical choice. More than just logical, she found herself longing for the warmth of his embrace, to feel his breath on her neck, his body against hers. She needed to be held, to be loved.

But there was still no answer.

She looked at the clock and realized that he could be driving and not able to respond. But then, a few seconds later, her phone rang. It was Steve.

"Oh, Steve," she said, when she slid the green 'answer' button to the right, "it's so good to hear from you!"

"Rachel," Steve said. She noticed his voice sounded a little tense. "Honey, I'm so sorry," he said quietly. "Uh, . . . I'm afraid my situation has changed." A few more seconds passed as Rachel's eyebrows bunched together. "I'm engaged. I'm getting married in April."

Rachel's eyes instantly filled with tears.

"Steve, I'm so happy for you," she said with a sincere smile, wiping away the tear.

"What's wrong?" he asked.

"Nothing," she replied, shaking her head vigorously. "Nothing at all. I can't be happier. Congratulations."

She disconnected before she could hear his response.

amien, I need to ask you something," Suzy said, holding her phone tightly against her ear. "Is there anything like an expulsion spell in your grimoire?"

"An expulsion spell?" he asked.

"Yes, a spell to actually get rid of a demon."

There was a long pause, and based on the images in her memory, Suzy could see Damien's forehead puckering as he thought about her question.

"To be honest," he said, "I don't know. The grimoire is written in some ancient dialect, and the person I had searching and translating it, well, maybe I should have been more specific. I asked her to find a spell that would render the spirit harmless to me and my family. Why? Do you think I've had what I needed all along?"

"Possibly," Suzy replied. "I'm afraid I'm no expert at ancient dialects. Any chance you can get your translator to look through it again?"

"Definitely," Damien said. "I'll call her tonight." After another pause, he asked, "Are you any closer to a decision?"

Suzy gave a pause of her own.

"I don't know," she finally said. "Still gathering intel." She sighed. "I still don't know what you think we can do."

"I know," Damien said, "you've told me you have no experience with this. And I understand your apprehension. But frankly, I'm just really damn impressed with your one hundred percent success rate."

"Success with ghosts, not so-called demons."

"I know, I get that."

"But, as I said," Suzy added, "I'm researching, considering my options."

"Fair enough. Thank you, Suzy. I appreciate you giving this fair and honest consideration. And I'll let you know what Amy says about an expulsion spell."

"Thanks, Damien."

She disconnected the call and looked at Fin, sitting on the other end of the sofa. He lifted an eyebrow. Suzy shrugged in response and put her phone down.

"That would sure make it easier if his book contains the necessary spell."

Fin nodded. He reached out a hand to her. Suzy didn't need any further invitation. She leaned toward him and snuggled into his arms, lying against his chest. They both sighed synchronously.

"How am I going to make this decision, Fin?"

"With the same wisdom and level-headed insight that you always do."

Suzy rolled her eyes and looked up at him, expecting to see a smartass grin on his face. He looked back at her very seriously.

"You're the most intelligent person I know," he explained, raising his eyebrows as if he were explaining the most obvious thing in the world. "You're smart and rational and brave. I've never known you to avoid making a decision just because it was hard."

"So," Suzy scoffed, "what you're saying is that you're not going to tell me what I should do."

"I don't *know* what you should do," Fin replied. "When I said you're the smartest person I know, I was including myself."

Suzy looked at him, a pained look on her face.

"I don't know whether to feel placated and flattered by that remark," Suzy said with a snarky smile, "or irritated at your complete lack of help."

Fin continued, grinning a little at her remark.

"What I *do* know is that, when the time comes, you will consider everything you know, all the information that you will have gathered, and you'll make the best possible decision under the circumstances."

Suzy settled back against Fin's chest, somewhat mollified. Then, she frowned.

"'Under the circumstances' is kind of a loaded phrase," she said with an apprehensive tone. "The best possible decision under the circumstances doesn't necessarily mean it's the best decision."

"That's the best any of us can *ever* do. Sometimes we just don't have all the information, but we have to make a decision anyway. And not to give Damien too much credit, but he was right about that back at the coffee shop. Under those circumstances, we have to rely, to an extent, on our gut."

"Our gut?"

"Take your best guess."

Suzy sighed.

"Fin, this is serious shit."

"I know it is. And I'm being completely serious. But, to paraphrase a line from *Star Trek IV: The Voyage Home*, I feel safer about your guesses than about most other people's facts."

"Hmm," Suzy said thoughtfully. She felt Fin's chest rise and fall with a few breaths. "So, you think I'm like Spock?"

"I think you're intelligent and logical, with a highly trained moral compass." He paused for a moment. "But you're definitely cuter." He pulled her closer. "And I gotta say that I'm kind of jazzed that you knew who was being referred to in the quote, enough that I know I'm not the only geek in the room."

» § «

Suzy didn't hear back from Damien until Friday.

"Suzy, I had Amy go through the grimoire again. It turns out it *does* contain a banishing ritual."

"Damien, that's great!" Suzy replied. "Have you tried it yet?"

There was a prolonged silence, and Suzy looked at her phone to make sure she was still connected.

"No," Damien finally said. "I mean, why would I? It's not time yet."

"I don't understand."

"Well, I told you last weekend that I'll be filming my series finale in November. That's when we'll try out the banishing ritual."

"But, what about your girls?" Suzy asked. "Aren't you concerned about them?"

"Of course, I am. That's why I used the binding spell in the first place. And for now, that's been working just fine. It's also why I called you. But if I perform the banishing ritual now, assuming it works, there won't be anything to film for the finale."

"But—"

"Suzy, I told you about my plan, and the reason for it. I want to leave behind a legacy, not just for my own admittedly voluminous vanity, but to bequeath a nice trust for my daughters. As long as the binding spell is working, as it has for the last few years, I'll keep it in place until November."

Suzy heaved a sigh, but she wasn't surprised.

"Alright."

A few moments passed before Damien spoke again.

"So," he continued hesitantly, "have you come any closer to a decision?"

Suzy closed her eyes. She had known the question would be coming, and she had known what her answer would be.

"Yes, Damien, I have." She opened her eyes and shook her head. "I'll do it."

17

I'm actually a little surprised," Rachel said. Suzy had gone to Rachel's house on Saturday for an afternoon tea. It was something that Rachel had instituted several years before, after Mark and Emma died, to keep Suzy from spending too much dark time alone. They had kept it up ever since then and did it on a regular basis.

"Why's that?" Suzy asked.

"Well, I just thought that you and Fin both seemed so dead set against Damien's plan."

"We still think it's a crazy idea. I mean parts of it I can definitely understand." She paused thoughtfully, her cup poised halfway to her mouth. "I've seen people die of cancer, and I can certainly understand him not wanting to go through that if it can be avoided. Physician-assisted suicide is legal in Maine, so I don't have a problem with that part of his plan." She took a sip.

"Although I think it's pretty creepy that he wants to do it on the air."

"Is that even legal?" Rachel asked. "Can you broadcast an actual death on TV?"

"I have no idea. And if not, I don't know if the laws are different for cable than they are for regular network TV. At any rate, I think it's pretty ghoulish."

Rachel nodded and quirked an eyebrow. Given her sympathy for Damien, Suzy was a bit surprised.

"I do think his motive for wanting to do this is a noble one," Suzy said. "Shannon and Claire are the sweetest girls, and I do respect his desire to take care of them after he's gone."

Rachel nodded, her eyes turning a little glossy.

"But that's also why I think he's a fucking idiot," Suzy continued.

"What do you mean?"

"He has an ancient grimoire, with a spell to actually get rid of this so-called demon. But he's putting off using it so he can do it on-the-air, as his last act on earth. So, what if it doesn't work? What if his daughters end up being unprotected, or worse, endangered by his actions?"

"The binding spell worked," Rachel replied, her voice a little shaky. "Why wouldn't the banishing spell?"

"We're talking about magic, Rachel." Suzy stopped and thought about what she was saying, and she shook her head. When she spoke again, her voice was lower, more level. "We're talking about a magic spell in the twenty-first century." She sighed. "I know I've had to swallow my pride and reverse my beliefs about this whole afterlife thing, but magic spells?"

Suzy looked at Rachel, and her expression changed.

"I'm sorry," she said. "I know you like him." She rolled her eyes and leered back at Rachel. "And I *know* he liked you! I mean, damn! The way you looked last weekend, if I didn't have Fin, you might have convinced *me* to swing that way."

Rachel blushed and looked down at her cup. She smiled, and felt a little warm, when she remembered Damien's eyes caressing her body at the coffee shop. Then, she remembered that he was dying, and her smile faded.

"I know what's different!" Suzy suddenly blurted out, jerking Rachel out of her momentary melancholy. "You got rid of a bunch of your tchotchkes!" Rachel looked up at Suzy and saw her looking around. She nodded and smiled.

"I did," she said. She took a deep breath, which seemed to engulf her dark mood. When she blew it out in a heavy sigh, she felt better. She did an odd frowning smile at Suzy. "I realized a few days ago that, like you always said, it was just too much to keep up with." She looked around, and the smile changed back into a confused frown. "It feels strange. It practically feels like I've cut off a part of me. But at the same time," she shook her head, "I feel almost relieved."

"Well," Suzy said, "you held on to it a lot longer than I could have."

"It just felt like it was time for a new me," Rachel said, and Suzy could hear the relief she had mentioned.

"Well, I don't know about that. I still kind of like the old you. But I can certainly see how this could take a bit of a load off."

They smiled at each other, and Rachel decided that this particular afternoon tea had been more for her than for Suzy.

§

After Suzy left, Rachel felt motivated by their conversation. She walked through a couple of rooms, rooms that she hadn't yet decluttered, looking at the various collections she had accumulated over the years.

As she looked at all the stuff, she remembered something that her mother had worried about. Something of a clutter bug herself, she had frequently lamented that she didn't want to leave such a mess for her children to have to deal with when she died.

Her mother was still alive, but as it turned out, Rachel and her brother *did* have to deal with it when they put their parents in an assisted living facility. Whatever their parents couldn't take with them, and that Rachel or Roger didn't want, was sold in an estate sale or donated.

Rachel did want a lot of it, though. It was her mother who had originally stoked her colonial-era fancy, and many of the items she had on display had come from her childhood home.

She thought now about her mother's regrets about leaving such a massive chore for her children.

Not a problem for me, she thought, bemoaning her non-existent love life. *Not even any prospects.*

She shook her head and focused again on her décor. She had a China cabinet full of memorabilia from Salem's days of witchcraft hysteria. She shuddered remembering that Fin had done what they called a sendoff of a ghost who had been the son of an accused witch in Salem. Her shudder was from, not only the chilling story that he and Suzy had told about it, but also about the horrific terror that all those poor people must have lived through back then.

She took a deep breath and nodded her head. It was historical. It was interesting. But she decided that it just wasn't her anymore.

That idea was shocking to Rachel. All of this had been her domestic identity for so long, she was amazed that her tastes — or, at least, her tolerance — had changed so drastically without her realizing it.

But there was also a definite measure of relief.

18

Suzy frowned, looking at the papers in front of her. She hadn't signed anything yet. Two weeks after their visit, Damien had flown his plane down from Bangor to visit with Suzy and Fin and get some paperwork prepared for his finale. They were sitting in the breakfast nook booth, Suzy and Fin together on one side, Damien on the other.

"I don't really understand how much there will be for me to do," Suzy said. "I don't know why you need us."

"Just backup," Damien smiled, then he looked a little embarrassed. "I already know how you feel about me and my show, but as I said, I *am* an experienced spiritist. However, I don't have any experience with this sort of thing."

"Neither do we," Fin said.

"Understood, but I'm thinking that, with the two of us," he glanced back at Suzy, "or the three of us, we can get the job done. Part of it," he put his hands up in a conceding gesture, "I readily admit, is marketing. I'm a name brand, and you SpiritSensors, I think, are getting to be a name brand, too. So, that will be a draw for the audience. Crossovers are really popular. But there's also the matter of strength in numbers."

"Why don't you just get a priest to come in and do an exorcism?" Suzy asked. Damien shook his head.

"I thought about it once. But I'm not a religious man, not anymore. Neither is my show. I mean, it's not like Catholics are the only ones who have these issues."

"No," Fin said, "but *The Exorcist* was very popular with people of various faiths, or *no* faith."

"That's true, but I try to be faithful to myself and to my own beliefs, and I try to keep my show entirely secular."

"I'm not sure you understand," Suzy said, easing the topic back to one of her concerns. "My participation will be pretty much invisible to viewers. It'll just look like I'm sleeping. Not exactly riveting TV."

"Why is that?" Damien asked, his eyebrows puckered.

"Because I connect to the spirit, see what they see. It's like I'm in a trance while we're connected."

"Really?" The rest of his face joined his eyebrows in being puckered.

"Yeah, I thought you understood what I did."

"Well, not in detail, I guess. Can't you just expel it?"

"That's not the way it works. Not for me, anyway. When I'm in the episode, I try to motivate them to leave of their own accord, rather than forcing them."

"Seems like a dangerous thing to do with a demon."

"If it even comes to that," Suzy said. She still felt that he was overstating his case, but she kept that part to herself. "But you're confident in the banishing spell you have."

"I am," he nodded.

"In which case my presence will likely be superfluous."

"Okay," Damien replied, sounding frustrated. "But, just in case, as I said, I'd like to have backup."

"So, you can film me sleeping?"

"I understand," Damien nodded thinking. "Maybe . . . maybe Fin can provide color, a little background narration, whatever, while you're in — what did you call it? — your episode."

"If I did," Fin said, "it likely won't have anything at all to do with what she's experiencing, because I won't know, either. Not unless I'm connected to this spirit at the same time."

"Can you do that?" Damien asked, tilting his head curiously.

"No idea," Fin replied, hoping his voice and expression transmitted how much he did *not* want to try it. "We've only managed it once, and even then, it was kind of unintentional. And it wouldn't be any more exciting for the viewers than if it was just Suzy. Then, you'd have *two* unconscious people on camera instead of just one."

"Okay," Damien said undeterred, "well, my shows are not live. I'm sure my editors will be able to make it interesting. Especially in post-production, after you've revealed what you experienced. Maybe some reenactments or something like that."

Suzy squinted, feeling her pro/con list being tilted just a little more toward "con."

"It'll be fine," Damien insisted, seeing her hesitance. "You will have final say concerning anything having to do with your image and depiction."

"Really?" Fin asked.

"Absolutely," Damien replied, reaching forward and shifting papers around. He pulled one out. "That's what this form is about."

Suzy and Fin looked over the paper. They glanced at each other, and the glance turned into a gaze. After an almost imperceptible mutual nod, Suzy sighed and reached for the pen.

As they signed various papers, Damien gathered them, replacing them with others.

"And this is just a standard non-disclosure agreement," Damien said, placing identical sheets of paper in front of Suzy and Fin, the last ones in his arsenal, "stating that you won't discuss anything having to do with the episode with anyone until it airs."

He was all smiles as the last of the documents were made official.

"Excellent!" he said, tapping the papers into an orderly stack. He slipped them into the leather briefcase which looked somewhat incongruous dangling at the end of his bare, tattooed arm. "I'm anxious to get started on this case and, well, at the same time, I'm dreading it." His smile faded as he got to the end of the sentence.

Suzy and Fin seemed to share the dread, but without his enthusiasm.

"I just hope that, somehow, we're successful," Suzy said ominously.

» § «

"Hi, Damien," Rachel said when she opened her door early that afternoon. "Come in."

Damien smiled as he shook her hand. Since he had his briefcase in his left hand, his handshake this time was not the two-handed variety.

"Thank you, Rachel," he said, regarding her with the intense scrutiny and consideration that she had come to know during their weekend at his house.

When Damien called that morning to let her know that he was coming, Rachel had chosen not to wear anything particularly sexy or attractive this time, opting instead for the worn jeans and the flannel shirt she had already been wearing as she continued paring down the décor in her home.

While she had felt at the time of their trip to Maine that she had chosen the right ensemble, she later decided that she had overdone it. Even though she didn't know if desperation had entered Damien's mind when he looked at her, it definitely did hers.

She knew that she tended to overthink things sometimes, and she couldn't be certain if this was one of those times or not. In fact, it had been on her mind so much that it was the first thing she mentioned.

"Damien, I'm sorry if I seemed inappropriate when we met."

Damien frowned as if he didn't know what she was talking about. She had hoped he would have simply nodded and smiled and said it was okay, and that nothing more needed to be said about it. Now, further embarrassed, she knew that something more needed to be said about it.

"I was just starstruck and wanted to make a good impression on you. I chose an outfit that, I think now, was not appropriate for the situation. I have a feeling I may have looked as if I was trying too hard. I'm sorry, I just wanted to look attractive."

"You *were* attractive," he smiled. "You were beautiful." His eyes slid down her body and back up, and she felt the same tingle she had felt back in the coffee shop. "You're beautiful now."

"Pfsh," Rachel scoffed. She put her arms out at her side and looked down at her jeans and her flannel shirt. When she did, she realized that, as she had been working during the day, her shirt had come unbuttoned a little farther down than she wanted it. Seeing that, and overthinking again, she struggled with whether she should conspicuously button the next button or just leave it.

As she was trying to decide, the thought came to mind that she might need to call Steve for comfort after Damien left.

Then she remembered. Steve was no longer available to her.

Her attention snapped back to Damien when he touched her arm.

"Rachel," he said, his voice soft, yet deep and resonant, "you're a beautiful woman. The sooner you accept that fact, the happier you'll ultimately be."

Flushed and flustered, she cleared her throat and motioned toward the living room.

"Come on in here," she said, walking toward the sofa. He followed her and they sat down.

Damien reached into the briefcase and pulled out a single sheet of paper and placed it on the coffee table in front of them.

"Okay," he said, "I know you're not going to be involved in my finale, but since you were there when we were discussing it, the network's lawyers have informed me that they think you still need to sign a non-disclosure agreement."

"Of course," Rachel nodded. She quickly read the form, then signed it. "And you usually take care of all the paperwork yourself?"

"No, not usually," he replied, slipping the paper back into the briefcase and snapping it closed. "Only under special circumstances."

"And this qualifies as a special circumstance?" she asked, a combination of amusement and confusion displayed on her face.

"It is," Damien said, turning back to her. His gaze was intense, his meaning clear, eliminating any confusion she may have felt before. As she peered at his face, though, she saw that, while his meaning was clear, there was some indecision below the surface.

He sighed and pushed on.

"I really struggled for a few days after you left," he continued, looking downward, as if he had to pull his gaze away from her face in order to concentrate. "My mind has been like a crazy ping pong game for the last couple of weeks."

Rachel frowned as Damien peered downward, concentrating on his hands.

"I've always been a romantic," he continued. "I admit I like women, and I like having female companionship. But since I don't want to leave a trail of pain and sadness in my wake, I haven't been pursuing any romantic relationships since I received the diagnosis."

He sighed and looked up at Rachel.

"But, Rachel, I haven't been able to get you out of my head. I see your face when I wake up and when I go to sleep, and to some extent, at all points in between. And since, it seemed to me, that you were attracted to me, as well, I finally decided," he hung his head in shame, "selfishly, perhaps, to leave it up to you."

Rachel's eyes burned and tears rushed in to relieve the discomfort. She reached for Damien's hand and felt his fingers close desperately around hers.

"Damien," she replied, her voice little more than a whisper, "yes, I am *so* attracted to you. And I can't—"

She stopped and took a breath, blowing it out before continuing.

"At the risk of sounding self-centered, I can hardly believe that I've found someone that I'm attracted to, and who is attracted to me, but who only has two months to live." Her voice cracked as she said the words, and a tear broke free, tumbling down her cheek.

"But it's not just about me," she insisted. "My heart breaks for you, and for your precious girls."

Damien leaned toward her, and Rachel met him in the middle, their foreheads touching.

"It's so unfair," he said. Rachel nodded, feeling his head rocking up and down with hers. "I don't want to hurt you, but . . . but I also don't want to die knowing that the woman who is perfect for me could have been a part of my life, even for a short time. If she wanted to."

"I do," Rachel whispered.

Damien pulled his head away from Rachel's enough to look in her eyes.

"Are you sure?" he asked, using his free hand to push her blondish hair away from her face. In answer, she reached up and grasped him by the back of the neck, pulling his head toward her and pressing her mouth against his.

Their tongues probed hungrily for each other, and she wrapped her arms around him, pulling him against her. When they finally broke free, she looked in his eyes.

"Yes," she said, "I'm sure."

Damien tugged her back against him, burying his face in her neck. But Rachel pulled away, allowing herself to fall to the side on the sofa. Damien followed her down, resting on an elbow. His forearm under her neck, he pushed the hair in his ponytail back over his shoulder. Caressing her cheek, he looked deeply into her eyes for a few moments, and he saw acceptance.

He leaned down and kissed her lips again, more gently this time. He felt tears building in his eyes as he slipped his hand under her flannel shirt and under her bra, cupping his hand over her breast. He savored its softness, and the contrast of the hardening nipple against his palm. He felt her chest rising and falling under his hand, and the steady pounding of her heart racing.

His gentle reverie ratcheted up a few notches when he felt a groping light pressure at his crotch. Rachel fumbled blindly with the zipper of his jeans before tugging it downward.

Within just a few seconds, their clothing was off, or at least opened, and there was no more room for tears. Only ecstasy.

» § «

After the initial nascent urgency had eased, Rachel and Damien had moved upstairs to her bedroom. In the calm that had settled in after their frenzied lovemaking, Rachel was lying comfortably against Damien, with her head on his shoulder.

The sun was setting and the warm autumn light fading in the windows, and Rachel had to squint a little to make out the individual images that made up the intricate pattern of Damien's intertwined tattoos. He smiled indulgently as she did so.

She had initially asked, jokingly, if he was one of those "trendy" people who got an obscure Asian tattoo because he thought it was deep and philosophical, and he liked the look of it, without realizing that it actually meant something mundane like "boloney sandwich."

He assured her that he was well aware of all of their meanings.

"I give you my word, young lady," he had said in a mock insulted tone, his eyebrows raised offendedly, "none of my tattoos are about sandwiches."

She decided to put him to the test. So far, she was in the process of working her way up his left arm.

"And what's this one?" she asked, pointing at what looked like a squatting one-eyed stick figure with curved horns.

"*Monas Hieroglyphica,*" Damien replied. "That symbol was created by John Dee, an occultist who was the official alchemist and astrologer of Queen Elizabeth I. It represents a combination of the moon, the sun, the elements — as they knew them then — and fire."

"Hmm," Rachel said, raising an eyebrow. Her finger continued tracing the designs upward and settled at one on the front of his left shoulder, a seven-pointed star. "And this one?"

Damien lifted his arm so he could see what she was pointing at.

"It's a heptagram. That's a symbol that has meaning in a lot of different cultures. Judaism, Islam, paganism. In Wicca, it's known as the elven star."

Rachel's finger continued tracing the images up his shoulder. She had discovered earlier when his shirt came off that the tattoos were not just on his arms. The designs continued onto his chest, and her finger stopped at a familiar one.

"I've seen this one a lot," she said, "but I don't know what it is. It's Egyptian, isn't it?"

It was a cross, the crosspieces flared a bit at the ends, but the top vertical line was replaced with a droplet shape. In this case, the droplet was a little rounder than she had usually seen it, and it encircled his nipple.

As she traced the shape of the tattoo, Rachel took the opportunity to follow the circle around and tickle his nipple with her fingertip.

"That's called an ankh," he smiled. "Yes, it's ancient Egyptian, but it's been associated more recently with neo-paganism and the Goth subculture. It's a symbol of eternal life and rebirth."

"Okay," Rachel said in a conceding tone, settling her head back on his shoulder, "I guess you do know what they are." She looked up at his face, narrowing her eyelids suspiciously. "At least I assume you do. I have no idea if your answers were correct or not. You could just be pulling my leg."

"I would *never* pull your leg," he insisted, "except literally."

Rachel smiled. Damien reached over and grasped her buttock, pulling her closer against him, and kissed her.

"I noticed from your décor your own interest in history," he said.

"Well," Rachel said in an ambiguous tone as she glanced around her darkening room, "it's mainly early American history, and I'm currently in the process of paring it down." She looked back up at Damien and smiled. "But, please, do go on."

"It might interest you to know," he said, "that some ancient cultures used tattoos to keep magic spells handy, within easy reach, where they couldn't be misplaced.

"And even now, in several Asian countries, certain tattoos are believed to actually *contain* magic. These are called yantra tattoos, and they supposedly contain magical spells to bless or protect their wearers, or to affect those around the wearer, to make them feel a certain way about him. To magically make an enemy or opponent fear him, for instance."

"Hmm," Rachel said suspiciously, "you don't have a tattoo somewhere on here to make me fall in love with you, do you?"

Damien lifted his head to look at her and she immediately cringed, realizing that she had said more than she meant to say. When he smiled, though, and shook his head, she sighed softly.

"No, sweetheart," he said quietly, "I don't have anything like that." They passed a few seconds silently breathing against each other's bodies before he spoke again. "No, if I thought magic tattoos were real, I probably wouldn't need Suzy and Fin."

That statement brought back to Rachel's mind the reason for his being here in Boston, and what the near future held for him. The darkness in her room suddenly became considerably gloomier. She didn't want to be reminded that she had literally only days to spend with this man.

She sighed and snuggled closer to him.

19

God, I feel so unprepared," Suzy said, gazing out the picture window across the harbor. The sky was a bright cloudless blue and the golden and scarlet foliage was dropping everywhere. Autumn had always been Suzy's favorite season in Marblehead, and she felt as if she was missing it. "We're filming that damn show in two days, and I don't really know any more than I did when he first asked us."

"I know," Fin replied, rubbing his face vigorously with his palms. He looked at Suzy. "So, are you feeling more apprehensive about this demon idea now?"

Suzy took a few moments to think before responding.

"I don't know. I mean this whole stupid thing sounds like a plot for a horror movie. I can't believe I ever agreed to it. For god's sake, this is the twenty-first century. We're supposed to be beyond all that fearful superstitious mumbo-jumbo by now."

They had both spent the last several weeks doing extensive research on expelling a demon, and had gleaned little more than a long list of apocryphal anecdotes and religious rituals.

"Although, you're not, really," Fin added. Suzy turned and looked at him with a puzzled expression. "Unprepared," he clarified. "You got information from Lilith, a source you trust implicitly, and which has been corroborated by a few of the other sources we found."

"I know," Suzy sighed, turning back to the window, "but that feels like so little."

"What about . . ." Fin stopped, gazing out the window, his face displaying his concentration. He looked at Suzy.

"You learned last year that Emma is your spirit guide. What about asking for her help?"

Suzy snickered.

"So much for our advanced twenty-first century maturity."

Suzy thought about Fin's question, but then shook her head.

"No, Emma made it clear to me that, that first contact notwithstanding, she wouldn't be able to make herself visible to me or physically intervene in my life. I can't sit down with her and discuss our plans and have her tell me what I should do. Like everyone else's spirit guide, from that point on, she'll just be able to provide nudges in the right direction, and I'll have to try to make the best decision possible and hope for the best."

"Then, that's what you do," Fin said.

"And what if it doesn't work?"

"Then, if there *does* seem to be something to it, we need to be prepared to get the hell out of there, the show be damned."

Suzy turned back, nodding her head, and sat down next to Fin.

"Just in case, I don't want Julie anywhere near there when we're doing that." Suzy pondered a moment. "Maybe we can get a hotel. I wonder if Rachel wants to go up there with us again. Maybe she can stay with Julie while we're playing John Constantine."

"Good idea," Fin smiled. "And good use of a pop cultural reference."

Suzy smiled back at him as she lifted her phone off the coffee table. Rachel picked up after two rings.

"Hey, girlfriend," Suzy said. "How are you? I haven't heard from you in a few days."

"I'm fine," Rachel replied, drawing it out a little hesitantly. Suzy lowered her eyebrows, feeling a combination of curiosity and suspicion.

"Okay," she said, matching Rachel's tone and pacing. She decided to ask her intended question, and then see if Rachel opened up after that. "We were wondering if you might want to go with us up to Bangor on Friday. Frankly, we could use a babysitter while we're doing our thing." She tried to keep her voice steady as she quelled the shiver she felt when she thought of their reason for going there, and how close the time was.

"No," Rachel said.

Suzy was just about to thank her, but then she realized that she had given the exact opposite response than the one she was expecting.

"No?"

"I'm sorry, Suzy. I'm . . . I'm already in Bangor."

"You — huh?"

Rachel heaved a heavy sigh.

"I decided that I needed to take a couple of weeks off from work. I've spent the last few days in Bangor with — with Damien."

It was a few seconds before Suzy realized that, despite the fact that her mouth was hanging open, she hadn't uttered any words.

"You're with Damien?" she finally asked.

She felt a slight movement and turned to see Fin looking curiously at her.

"We've been seeing each other for the last few weeks," Rachel explained.

"Rachel, I — I had no idea. Why didn't you say anything about that?"

"Because I know how you and Fin feel about him. Frankly, I didn't want to ignite further criticism of him, or me, for that matter."

Rachel's tone was not overly accusatory, but the words dug a little into Suzy's conscience.

"Honey, I would never try to make you feel bad about anyone you were interested in."

"I know," Rachel replied. Her voice was lower now, as if Damien was nearby and she didn't want him to hear. Or she was struggling to keep her feelings in check. "But still you and Fin were pretty outspoken about him when we first met him."

"I'm sorry. I—well, I'm afraid our opinion of him hasn't changed, but we'll try to keep them in check. Still, we love you, Rachel. I'm sorry you felt like you had to keep this to yourself."

"You just don't know him as I've come to know him during the last few weeks."

"I'm sure that's true. And to be honest, our opinion of him is purely professional, not personal. I don't know if that makes a difference or not, but if he makes you happy, then I'm happy for you."

"Thank you," Rachel replied, her voice relaxing a bit.

"Wait," Suzy said, "you said you took a couple of weeks off from work, but you've only been up there for a few days."

Then, realization struck as soon as she had completed her observation.

"I'm going to need some time afterwards," Rachel said quietly.

"Of course," Suzy groaned. "Sweetie, you know I'll be here for you, as much as you were for me after Mark and Emma."

"I know."

A few moments of silence passed between them before Suzy spoke again.

"Okay," Suzy took a long breath and exhaled nervously, "well, I guess we'll see you on Friday."

"Okay, Suzy. And thank you."

After disconnecting, Suzy sighed and sat back on the sofa, stunned.

"She's been seeing Damien for weeks now."

"I heard," Fin replied.

"Probably since he came down here to have us all sign those papers."

Fin nodded, absently petting Ursula. Several moments passed as they processed the information.

"I need to talk to Damien," Suzy finally said.

» § «

"Damien, I can't even begin to express to you how apprehensive I'm feeling about this crazy show of yours," Suzy said on the phone.

"I'm sorry, Suzy. What can I do?"

"I have no idea. *I* don't know what to do. But I'm feeling almost like I need to say no to this."

A few moments of silence passed before Damien responded.

"Suzy, you can't back out now. We start filming in two days. You're contractually obligated."

"I feel like my life is a little more important than a signed contract," Suzy replied indignantly. She felt as if she was exaggerating her concerns, but she didn't like feeling backed into a corner and wanted to make her point.

"Of course it is," Damien said conciliatingly. "I didn't mean to imply otherwise." A moment passed and Damien continued with a completely different tone of voice. "Wait, I thought you didn't even believe in demons."

"I'm not sure I do," Suzy conceded. "Which further suggests that I not do this. Not only will I not be any help to you, but I could even be damaging my own reputation as a reputable spiritist."

Damien gave an audible sigh.

"Okay, you and Fin have both made your feelings known about my own validity. Point taken. Multiple times.

"But you signed an agreement. You have to understand that I'm under the gun timewise. It's not like I can just put this on the back burner for an indefinite amount of time waiting for you to feel better about it."

"I know," Suzy replied, her voice tightening. "But I think that, if the tables were turned, you'd choose your own family over mine."

"Why are you suddenly so apprehensive about this?" Damien asked.

"It's not sudden at all," Suzy replied. "I've been feeling this ever since we first talked about it in the coffee shop."

"I remember you thought it was a load of bullshit."

"That's true," Suzy admitted, "and I admit that I'm still of that opinion. But I've also decided that I want to cover my bases, just in case there does end up being something to this."

"Understood. But you agreed to do it and signed the contract. What's changed?"

"I just don't feel prepared. I still don't know hardly anything about getting rid of an alleged evil spirit."

"Fair enough." Damien paused. "What can I do to make you feel better about it?"

Suzy took several breaths, trying to give herself time to gather her thoughts.

"I'm concerned about our safety, I mean if there is such a thing as a demon haunting your house. Not just *my* safety, but especially Fin and Julie. I don't want to have my family within reach when we're trying to expel this entity."

"Well, that's easy enough to fix," Damien replied without hesitation. "There are several outbuildings on my property. One of them is like a carriage house. I had it built as a sort of mother-in-law apartment for when Kate's mother came to visit. You and your family can stay there, away from the house."

Suzy spent a few moments pondering that possibility. While she was in the main house filming the episode, Fin could stay with Julie in the apartment. That eased her worries a little.

"And," Damien continued, "the first thing we'll do is the banishing spell." He sighed. "It may make for a pretty short and uninteresting show, but the binding spell worked. I have no doubt the banishing spell will work, too."

And, as Fin said, Suzy thought to herself, if things went south, she could just get the hell out of there.

She decided not to say anything about that.

"Alright, Damien," she finally sighed, "I guess we'll see you on Friday."

20

The gates didn't open for Fin automatically. He had to stop at the keypad and enter the code that Damien had sent them. As the massive oaken gates started swinging inward, he raised an eyebrow at Suzy and sighed.

"You ready for this?" he asked. Suzy just rolled her eyes at him.

He followed the gravel road through the gate but then, based on Damien's instructions, turned off to the right. This gravel road curved around the castle and led behind it to a charming little grim and grey storybook structure, styled similarly to the castle, but with flower beds around it. The flowers, alas, were dead now, but there were several maples and pines around the carriage house which provided a riot of autumn color.

Suzy smiled as she looked at where they would be staying for the next couple of days.

"It's beautiful."

Fin's love of old, historical things was activated by the sight, despite the fact that he knew it was only a modern replica.

"It is," he nodded.

He stopped in front of the carriage house and turned off the car. After the long drive, they were slow to get moving, but Suzy eventually opened her door.

"Oh my god," she groaned as she pulled herself out of the car, "I can't feel my butt."

"Well, bring it over here, babe," Fin replied. "I'll be happy to feel it for you."

Suzy cast a sneer over her shoulder toward Fin as he stood up on his side of the car, but the sneer softened as she realized that his suggestion didn't sound so bad. Maybe later.

Suzy unfastened Julie's car seat, smiling as the baby made cooing and gurgling sounds at her, while Fin gathered their luggage. They each carried their cargo into the little house. Suzy took Julie out of the car seat, opting to carry her in her arms, and she and Fin spent a few minutes looking around.

It really was a delightful little place, with fresh-cut flowers in vases at various locations throughout the suite. They were obviously from a florist, since all the flower beds were bare.

Despite the size of the little house, it was decorated grandly, similarly to their bedchamber in the main castle two months before. Tapestries hung from the walls, and a brocade fabric draped around the tester of their four-poster bed.

Against one wall, under beautifully carved arches of dark wood, were numerous built-in bookshelves packed with books and archaic doodads. Shields with crossed swords, axes and other medieval weapons were displayed on another wall.

For some reason, the thought of Damien's wife lying dead in the master bedroom of the main castle popped into Suzy's head, and she wondered when his mother-in-law had last visited.

She was startled by a knock at the door, and was relieved that the surprise dissipated her dark thoughts. She turned as Fin pulled the door open and found Rachel standing there.

"I could use your help," Rachel said.

> § «

"What are you doing, Damien?" Fin asked after Rachel led him into Damien's studio. The expansive room was saturated with sadness, the air charged with an almost tangible depression. The ghost hunter, sprawled in his chair, turned bleary eyes toward Fin, a glass in one hand and a bottle in the other.

Damien slipped into his deeper "eloquent narration" voice.

"I'm drowning my sorrows in the bottom of a bottle of hazy, unfulfilled dreams."

The effect was not quite as impressive due to the slurring of his words.

"That's an expensive drowning," Fin said, eyeing the bottle of 15-year-old Macallan.

"What, you think I should be saving my money for my old age?"

"That's not for me to say," Fin shook his head and shrugged, sinking into the chair opposite him. "Just an observation."

"Grab a glass."

"No, thanks," Fin said quietly. "It's still a little early in the day for me."

"I'm on the threshold of entering my last fucking day on earth," Damien said indignantly. "You should drink with me."

"Nah, I just don't want to encourage that kind of behavior."

Damien cocked his head at Fin, raising his eyebrows in offense.

"What kind of behavior? You're judging me for having a last drink?"

"I'm not judging," Fin replied. "Truth be told, if I was in your situation, I don't know how well I'd handle it."

He shook his head thoughtfully.

"For a sane person, someone who enjoys life, I think what you're about to embark on takes a special kind of bravery. To say goodbye to everything you love in this world and intentionally cross the veil into the next one," Fin raised his eyebrows and nodded, "that takes balls."

That seemed to mollify Damien a bit. He relaxed his own eyebrows and took a drink. Then, he leveled his gaze, to the best of his ability, at Fin.

"Are you just trying to make up for saying you thought my plan was crazy?"

"Not at all. We still think your plan is absolutely batshit."

Damien snickered and took another drink.

"I mean that's pretty much why we reluctantly agreed to take part in it in the first place," Fin continued. "We don't want your girls' fate left in the hands of an unmitigated fucking lunatic."

Damien sighed and shook his head.

"Are you enjoying this?" he asked.

"A little," Fin said, his eyes crinkling a bit.

Damien smiled scornfully at Fin. He rolled his eyes, and then appeared to be a little dizzy from the motion. He moved his glass toward his lips, then seemed to think better of it.

"Those girls deserve a loving father who'll be there for them," Fin continued, "at least to the extent that he's able to do so. I guess it's a good thing James is going to be there to be that father."

He could see the anger on Damien's face before he exploded.

"You son of a bitch! You don't know shit about how I feel about my girls."

"Well, that's not entirely true. You've spoken about how you feel about them. And the fact that you came to us for help in the first place, and your stated reason for doing so, that kind of tells me how you feel."

That brought Damien up short, and he didn't seem to know how to respond.

"I do know, though," Fin continued softly, "that if I only had one day left to live, I'd want to spend it with the people who meant the most to me. And I'd want to be completely clear-headed when I did."

Damien looked at Fin, apparently struggling to process the thought. He drew in a deep shuddering breath and blew it out.

Fin, just a few feet in front of him, tried not to react too visibly to the smell.

Bunching his brows together, Damien placed the bottle and the glass on the end table next to his chair.

» § «

After a hot shower and two strong cups of coffee, Damien wasn't sober, but he was, at least, a little more alert. He joined Fin, Suzy and Rachel in a room that seemed like a semi-modern living room, despite the stone and the high ceilings and the pseudo-candle chandeliers and the medieval décor.

Fin and Suzy were sitting in a plush, sunken, 70s style conversation pit, with Julie on Suzy's lap, cooing and gurgling. Damien's girls were sitting next to them, and Claire was particularly happy that the baby was awake. Rachel sat on the other side of the girls, a comforting arm resting around Shannon's shoulders, while a fire blazed in an enormous fireplace in front of them.

"Daddy!" Claire exclaimed as she jumped up from the opulent sofa and ran up out of the seating pit to Damien. Julie looked around surprised at the sudden and boisterous departure of her recent admirer.

Fin saw the tears in Damien's eyes as he swept Claire into his arms. He cast a quick glance at Shannon and saw tears in her eyes, as well.

While Fin didn't know how much Claire knew, at this point, about Damien's upcoming date with infinity, he did know that Shannon was aware of his plans.

Fin had attended funerals in the past, but he had never actually seen someone die. He was glad that his personal assignment was to stay with Julie in their carriage house apartment. And that fleeting thought made him fervently

hope that Damien's plans did not include having his daughters present when he died.

» § «

They all had a quiet dinner together that night. Moods
were light and happy, on the outside, at least. While all but
the youngest were aware of what would be happening the
next day, they all valiantly kept those feelings tamped down
for the evening.

21

Damien and Rachel had a long, elaborate breakfast with Clair and Shannon. Daryna, the *au pair*, never asked why Damien wanted such a big breakfast. She simply followed his orders and cooked the eggs and bacon and pancakes and hash browns and English muffins.

The mood around the table was a difficult mix. Damien, Rachel and Shannon were aware of what the day ahead held in store. Claire was blissfully oblivious and talked non-stop, but Damien seemed to love it.

After breakfast was over and Daryna had cleared all the dishes, Damien instructed Shannon and Claire to get their coats.

"I have a busy day here," he told them, "and Daryna's going to take you to town for the day."

Shannon looked at him critically as her little sister ran to get her coat. There were tears in her eyes.

"Dad, are you sure about this?"

Damien sighed and nodded, grasping her shoulders.

"Yes, honey, I am. I don't have much time left as it is. If I don't nip it in the bud, I'm going to be screaming in pain, which won't be any fun for me, obviously, or for you and Claire. I don't want you remembering me that way."

Shannon blinked, sending the tears tumbling down both cheeks.

Damien pulled her in for a hug, and Shannon wrapped her arms around him, holding him tighter than she had in a long time.

Claire came pounding back, tugging her coat on, and looked curiously at them.

"What are you doing?" she asked.

"Just saying goodbye," Damien replied lightly.

He let go of Shannon and knelt down to hug Claire. Claire hugged him back, but she seemed a little baffled by his attention.

"Daddy, we're only going into town. We'll be back this afternoon."

"I know, sweetie," Damien replied. "I'm just missing you already," he added in a lighter tone. He smiled at her as she pulled away.

» § «

Julie was in her carrier on the bed in the carriage house watching Fin and Suzy eat their breakfast. Fin had driven into town and brought back bagels and coffee.

Julie was jabbering, repeating "ba-ba-ba" over and over, interspersed occasionally with a raspberry. Fin turned to look at her.

"Thanks, Julie," he said, "now I'm going to have that tune stuck in my head all day."

Suzy smiled, at his joke, but also at the baby, and Julie smiled back at her, excitedly waving her arms up and down.

"God," Suzy sighed, "I just want to stay here with you guys." She looked at Fin, already knowing the answer to her tongue-in-cheek question. "Do I really have to do this?"

"Based on all the papers we signed, babe, I'm afraid you do."

"What if I say it was my evil twin?" Suzy suggested excitedly. "She waited until I was out and she infiltrated our home. She's the one who signed that contract, not me, so I'm not legally obligated."

"Wouldn't work," Fin said, shaking his head. "She could never fool me."

"Oh?"

"Yeah. She's hot!"

Suzy smiled and scratched her nose with her prominently extended middle finger.

"Fine," she said, standing up.

Julie responded by extending her hands, her fingers grasping the air toward Suzy.

"Oh," Suzy groaned.

Fin stood and lifted Julie out of her carrier.

"Sorry, sweetie," he said, "Mama can't take you. She has to deliver us from evil."

Suzy rolled her eyes, but she took Julie's hands in hers and planted several kisses on her cheeks.

She looked up at Fin and kissed him.

"Hopefully, I can get away at lunchtime."

Fin smiled and nodded, as Suzy walked out the door.

hones off!" shouted Damien. The hubbub in the studio quieted slightly as people began giving attention to their cell phones.

James leaned toward Rachel and Suzy.

"Damien's really strict about no interruptions or distractions during filming in the studio." He pointed toward a table near the door where a few cell phones already lay, and others were being deposited.

Damien's home studio was more crowded than Suzy had seen it before. Besides Damien, James and Terry, along with Rachel and Suzy, several others were there, as well, primarily producers and technicians of various disciplines.

Suzy and Rachel made their way toward the table, turning off their phones and leaving them there with the others. Seeing the numerous nearly identical black phones arranged there, Suzy was glad hers was the only one with a red cover.

She turned around and looked back at the room. The activity was ongoing, though the volume had reduced slightly. Despite the flurry, she could also sense a heaviness, a dark mood.

Suzy knew that this was often the case when filming the final episode of a show. The cast and crew had spent the previous seasons becoming something like family, and now, the family was going their separate ways.

But she knew this was different. Damien was right. She had never heard of the main star of a popular show actually killing himself on camera. Knowing that he was dying, and was going to go by his own hand, had to be weighing more heavily on many of them than just filming a final episode.

She saw Damien standing near his chair, and he raised his hand to get her attention, motioning her over to his personal set. Most of the people were over there, now, standing behind the cameras and lights, and Rachel followed, to get out of the cameras' range.

Suzy looked at Rachel as they made their way across the room. Her face looked dazed, as if her emotions were stretched too tightly. Suzy gently put her hand through the crook of Rachel's arm.

Rachel looked at Suzy, her eyes glossed with tears that had been lurking just below the surface. She squeezed Suzy's hand and nodded as they reached the set, Suzy separating to join Damien.

The furniture at his set had been rearranged. His chair was still central, but the loveseat had been pulled closer to it on the right, and one of the other chairs was now directly on the left. As Damien took his seat, James and Terry sat down on the loveseat, while Suzy sat on the chair, squinting into the bright studio lights.

She looked at Damien. His face was difficult to read. She could see the excitement that he always seemed to put into the discussion and execution of his work, but there seemed to be a tautness to it, as well, and a dazed quality similar to that on Rachel's face.

He tilted his head back and drew in a deep breath. As he let it out, he seemed a little more relaxed.

"Quiet, everyone," he called out. As the talking abruptly stopped, Suzy realized that he was also the director of his own show. "Roll cameras."

» § «

"Good evening, DeadWatchers," Damien said into the camera, his voice transmitting a little less enthusiasm than usual. "Welcome to the last episode of *King of the Dead*. That's right, this will be the final installment, for reasons I'm about to reveal to you now.

"I've been diagnosed with *glioblastoma multiforme*. That's medical-speak for an aggressive brain tumor which is inoperable and stubbornly resistant to radiation and chemo."

James reached over and squeezed Damien's shoulder.

"Since I've been given only a short time to live, and the last portion of that in pain and agony, I've decided to make use of the Death with Dignity Act and meet the end on my own terms. That means that, by the time this episode is over, I will have crossed the veil into the next plane. But before I do, I have work to do here.

"Seated on my right is Suzy MacKinley. A few of you may recognize her from her brief brushes with fame as the founder of the SpiritSensors. Along with her husband, Fin, she investigates hauntings and sends ghosts into the light."

Suzy cringed a little at the simplifying of what she does, but this was Damien's show. She wasn't here to promote herself, so she didn't bother to correct or expand on his description.

"I've asked Suzy here to help me out with my final job. For the last several years, I've had an evil spirit here in my home. A few years back, I placed a binding spell on it, so that it wouldn't cause any problems for my family.

"However, since I'll be leaving this earthly realm, and since I don't know if that will break the spell or not, and since I have little experience with demons, I've asked Suzy here to help me get rid of it."

"I think it should be noted," Suzy said, then she reached an apologetic hand toward Damien, "sorry for the interruption, that I don't have any experience with them, either."

"Should make for an interesting show all around," Terry muttered cynically.

"My hope," Damien said, his smile coming a little easier, "is that with our combined knowledge and skills, we can overpower this demon and kick its ass back to hell!"

There was the enthusiasm and bluster that Suzy had been expecting. She only wished she could feel as confident.

When they cut from the intro, Suzy stood up, feeling confused as to what she should do or where she should go. She turned and apologized again to Damien for interrupting him, but he was gracious.

"That uncertainty at the outset was perfect. Terry was right. It should be an interesting show."

Suzy looked around, seeing several of the others milling around uncertainly, as well.

"Well," Damien said, "James is going to be shooting a lot around here today. I'll set up some of the scenes. Other times, he'll just wander around shooting what could be used for personal interest." Suzy nodded. "I did promise that I'd try to do the banishing spell first thing. So, that'll be our next scene."

23

James always felt much more comfortable behind the camera than in front of it, so he was happy when Damien started moving around his studio space. Hoisting his camera onto his shoulder, James followed Damien to a small table that was arranged like an altar with old world magical paraphernalia.

"Alright," Damien said, looking into the camera, "I promised Suzy that I would try the banishing spell first thing."

Suzy, standing beside James, nodded at Damien as he picked up a small piece of cedar wood from the table. He flicked a match to life and held it under the end of the wood until it flamed.

"Since neither of us know for certain what we're getting into, she thought it might be safer to at least try to banish the demon while it was still under the power of my binding spell."

He blew out the flame and waved the smoking cedar back and forth over the table.

"It's important," he explained, "to cleanse the area, and the tools, of any negative energy."

Suzy thought the ritualistic acts seemed suspiciously religious in nature, but she kept quiet. If the binding spell works, maybe there was something to it.

"Next, I'm going to take this black candle. Now, a lot of people think that this color is used for cursing, or black magic, as if black indicates evil.

"But black candles have been used for centuries for protection, and since we're using it to get rid of an evil spirit, that's exactly what we need.

"I've selected a black taper, one made of paraffin wax, since it burns the fastest. Since we're not out in the field, on location, I don't want to be waiting around all day to find out if the spell worked or not, while Terry ravages the food table."

"I heard that!" Terry shouted from across the room, at the food table. Suzy smiled at Terry, and she recognized a feeling of relief that this brief moment of humor had offered. Then, she turned her attention back to Damien.

"I've also cut it in half, for that same reason, and because we may need to perform this spell a second time, if it doesn't work with the binding spell in place. So," he picked up a small antique dagger, and James zoomed in on his hands, "I'll start by carving the object of this spell into the side of the candle while thinking intently about it, having the evil spirit firmly in mind as I do this, thinking about how it has negatively affected me. Since I don't know this spirit's name, I'll just carve the word 'DEMON' into the candle."

As James continued shooting, that's exactly what Damien did. Then, he put down the little dagger and picked up an ancient-looking glass vial.

"Next, I'll anoint the candle with vinegar. Vinegar is a cleansing fluid, and according to the spell, it doesn't require much."

He opened the top of the vial, pressed his finger on the top and upended it briefly. Holding the candle with the top facing away from him, he rubbed his vinegar-wetted finger along the word "DEMON," away from him. He repeated the action a couple more times until he was certain the word was sufficiently anointed.

He placed the candle in a pewter candle holder and lit the wick. The spell continued with his narration as he sprinkled black pepper over the flame of the candle, a few sparks jumping from it.

Then, he combined black pepper, cayenne pepper and flaked eucalyptus leaves in a small black cauldron, sprinkling each ingredient in a counterclockwise direction. He picked up an old tarnished silver spoon and stirred the ingredients together.

Next, he selected a large, dried bay leaf and an ornate fountain pen. On the underside of the bay leaf, he wrote the word "DEMON" as he had on the candle, being silent once again to get the object of the spell firmly set in his mind as he did so.

He touched the tip of the bay leaf to the candle flame, and it immediately ignited. He dropped it into the cauldron where a small, brief conflagration took place. In just a few moments, though, the flame was out, a spiral of smoke curling up toward the distant ceiling.

He placed the lid on the little cauldron, sliding it in front of the candle, which had, already, burned down through the "D."

"Now, we wait," Damien said.

James lowered the camera.

"And we're out," he said. "I'll circulate and do some human-interest shots." Damien nodded.

§

"How are you doing?" Suzy asked as she eased toward Rachel. Her friend looked tense. She took a deep breath, but seemed to have a hard time blowing it out.

"I—I'm just . . ." She huffed as she gathered her thoughts. "I'm astonished at how everyone's going about these proceedings as if this is just another day." She looked at Suzy, her eyes distorted from tears. "In a few hours, Damien's going to be dead."

"I know," Suzy nodded quietly. "This whole thing really is kind of surreal."

She placed a hand on Rachel's shoulder.

"Are you sure you should be here?" she asked.

"Where else should I be?" Rachel asked.

"Anywhere but here!" Suzy insisted. Rachel shook her head.

"No, the man I love is here, and my best friend is here. There's no place else I even *could* be."

"Whoa!" Suzy said, her eyes widening with surprise. "You love him?"

Rachel hastily brushed away the tears that escaped.

"I don't know," she replied impatiently. "I haven't let myself think too much about it, since I know how, and when, it's ending." More tears rolled down her cheeks and she wiped them away. "But I think so."

"Oh, honey," Suzy said, sweeping Rachel into her arms, letting her have her cry.

» § «

After the candle finally burned down to the pewter holder, Damien picked out the unburnt stub of the candle and dumped it into the miniature cauldron, into the ashes that were still there, then took it outside. He took a moment to determine the direction of the breeze and then walked far away from his house, James following him with the camera. He tossed out the contents of the cauldron, allowing the breeze to sweep it away.

When he got back inside, he nodded to Suzy. Suzy went to the chair that she had occupied when Damien did the intro to his show. Damien put up his hands for everyone to be quiet as Suzy settled into a comfortable position.

The stationary camera was rolling, but James still focused his camera on her, for a different angle.

Suzy had done this so many times, she could hardly believe that she had needed to focus so intently on a flame back when it all began. Now, all she had to do was get comfortable and close her eyes, and she could get into the proper frame of mind at a moment's notice.

Except that there was nothing there.

Could it have been that easy? She concentrated, thinking that Damien was going to be pissed that he didn't get an exciting episode out of it.

But then, there *was* something, a flicker, a slight tickling of her SpiritSense. She felt a tingle on the back of her neck, that creepy feeling that someone was watching her.

It was still here.

24

It's still here, Damien. I can feel it."

Suzy stood in a small circle with Rachel, Damien, Terry and James. James had his camera on his shoulder. Several moments passed as Damien looked at Suzy, weighing their options. Nobody wanted to say it, so Suzy did.

"I think you need to undo the binding spell."

Damien sighed heavily.

"You're talking about psychically connecting with this thing. Do you realize how dangerous that could be?"

"I do," Suzy replied, "and I'm not making this suggestion lightly. The psychic connection is what I do with ghosts. What I did over there," she pointed to the chair she had occupied a few minutes before, "that was to see if I could sense its presence. Believe me, I have absolutely no desire to see what's in a demon's head, if it even exists, and I'm prepared to get the hell out of here at a moment's notice if anything truly threatening starts happening."

Damien glanced at James, and realized that anything they didn't want in the final show could be edited out. He turned back to Suzy.

"What if it prevents you from leaving?" Damien asked.

"Has it ever attempted anything like that before?"

"Well . . . no, but —"

"Damien," Suzy interrupted, "I'm not sure what's responsible for your sudden concern for my safety. Don't get me wrong, I appreciate it. I admit I was a little pissed at you before for being so eager to put me in this spirit's hands But it doesn't look like you're going to get rid of this spirit if you don't release the binding spell, and then perform the banishment spell again."

"So," Terry interjected with a cautious tone, "what kind of shit are we talking about here? Early *Poltergeist* with crawling meat and spinning furniture, or end *Poltergeist* with the house getting sucked into the ground?"

"Come on, guys," Damien said, "this isn't a movie."

"I know," Terry balked, "but you're talking about releasing a demon. We've never dealt with that before."

"I have," Damien said, his hand absently going to the scar at the base of his skull. He looked at Terry and James. "Be ready to duck if anything flies at you."

Then, he focused on James.

"But be sure the camera is rolling at all times."

Damien turned back toward his little tabletop altar. James cast a glance at Suzy, then followed Damien.

"Are you absolutely sure about this, Suzy?" Rachel asked. "I've never seen him so worried."

"No offense, Rachel," Suzy replied, "but up until a few weeks ago, you've only ever seen whatever he was willing to share on his show with his fans."

» § «

Having reversed the binding spell, Damien quickly got to work on the banishment spell, duplicating his actions from earlier. Since he had already shot the entire banishment spell in detail, James now only shot bits and pieces, talking to Damien in between shots.

"How are you doing, man?" he asked.

"I'm fine," Damien shot back impatiently. "Why?"

"You just seem a little more uptight than usual."

"Oh, you think?" Damien replied. "I've just released a demon in my home, and in a few hours, I'm going to inject a drug into my veins that's going to literally kill me. I think you might be a little uptight, too."

"I know," James said in a conciliatory tone, "I'm sorry. I'm just concerned about you, buddy." He sighed. "Are you really sure about this? I mean, what if you have more than a couple of months left? You could have more time with your daughters than you realize."

"That's true. Or I could have less. And it doesn't matter, if the time I have with them is spent in profound agony. I don't want to go through that, and I don't want to put *them* through that."

"Okay," James nodded, "you're right." He lifted the camera again as Damien carefully placed the anointed candle with his carving into the holder and lit it.

He sprinkled the black pepper over the flame, raising little crackling sparks. Then he pushed the candle back near the wall, positioning it precisely, after which he began mixing up the combination of ingredients in the miniature cauldron.

James continued filming the ritual, moving to get different angles. Damien still seemed irritable, though, impatiently moving around as if to get out of James' way, or vice versa. James decided that, with the two instances of this ritual, he likely had plenty of footage. He moved away uttering a silent sigh at the quickly approaching end of his friend's life.

» § «

Suzy knew that, based on the morning's attempt, it would take about three hours for the last half of the paraffin taper to burn down for the second banishing spell. She decided it was a good time to slip out and feed Julie, and have some lunch with Fin.

She filled a plate from the food table and slipped out the front door. She noticed how full the circular driveway and courtyard area in front of the castle were now, filled with vehicles that had carried the production team here.

She turned to the left, following the path that led away from the driveway and toward the carriage house. Her breasts felt like they were about to pop, and she couldn't wait to get her baby in her arms.

"Yum," Fin said as he took the plate of goodies. Julie looked up at Suzy's entrance from a blanket on the floor and smiled.

"Has she eaten yet?" Suzy asked.

"I was just about to feed her some baby veggies, but I'm sure she'll prefer what you've got."

While Fin started sampling the *King of the Dead* catering, Suzy sighed as Julie started nursing.

"How's it going?" Fin asked, setting the plate down on the end table next to her. Suzy made a scoffing sound and shook her head.

"Damien's as irritable as Mariah Carey on the day after Christmas."

"Yikes," Fin replied. After a few seconds, he added, "I suppose he's allowed, seeing as how he's about to die. So," he cast a cautious look at her, "you haven't seen the demon yet?"

"No, not so far." She picked up a bacon-wrapped shrimp and popped it in her mouth. "I still felt a presence after the first banishment spell, so Damien released his binding spell and did the banishment spell again. The candle has to burn all the way down before we know if it worked. And that's where we are now."

"I'm glad," Fin said, his voice expressing relief, "but I wish it was all over and we were headed back home."

"I know," Suzy said, her voice pumped full of anxiety. "I just have to keep telling myself that we're doing it for those girls." She looked down at Julie, who was looking up at her, her eyes full of trust and confidence in her mother's protection.

Or so Suzy imagined.

> § <

She reluctantly left Fin and Julie after an hour. As she walked out the door of the little cottage, the empty plate in her hand, a bit of bright green caught her eye to the right of the main castle, and she followed it, instead of following her previous path around the left toward the driveway and the front door.

The green turned out to be the leg of a swing set, and Suzy stopped to look at it, and the other playground equipment, to ponder this further reminder of why she had agreed to do this. She marveled at the depth of a parent's love for their child.

She had originally balked at taking on this case, due partly to her disbelief in the evil spirit concept, but mainly due to her love for Julie. She didn't want to risk leaving Julie motherless, if there did turn out to be something to this whole evil spirit thing.

Now in the midst of doing the episode, she wanted to kick herself for not thinking of that detail until after she had signed the paperwork, but it was Shannon and Claire who had really made her realize that it was worth it.

They had already lost their mother, and were about to lose their father, as well. They obviously loved James, and vice versa, but he wasn't their parent.

That made her think of the amendment she and Fin had recently added to their wills, to assign custody of Julie to Rachel in the event that she and Fin died. She felt good about that decision, but the idea of that possible eventuality brought a tear to her eye, on Julie's behalf. Rachel seemed to love Julie almost as much as she did, and her feelings seemed to be returned by Julie.

But what would Julie's life actually be like in that event? As much as Rachel loved Julie, she could never replace the baby's mother and father.

And Suzy knew that this was the case with Shannon and Claire, too. They're old enough to remember their father, to remember his love for them, and to feel the lack of it after today.

Suzy wanted to do whatever she could to ease their burden, their intense loss.

She looked at the swing set, imagined the girls playing on it, and she smiled sadly at their life, their future.

She sighed, continuing around toward the front door.

hat's going on?" Suzy asked Rachel when she got back inside. Most of the production people were just standing around. James and Terry were sitting in chairs in the studio area.

"Not much," Rachel replied. "Just waiting for the candle to burn down."

Suzy looked toward the altar table against the wall and saw that the candle was a little less than half the height it had been when Damien lit it.

"Where's Damien?" Suzy asked, looking around at all the faces.

"I don't know." Rachel shook her head, her face creased by worry. "He seemed really irritable a while ago and left."

"Left?"

"Yeah, just stormed out the door. I started to follow him, but James stopped me. He said he'd had a little clash with Damien earlier, and that Damien just needed some space."

Suzy noted Rachel's nervousness and the wringing of her hands, her eyes darting around the room.

"How are *you* doing?" she asked. Rachel's eyes snapped to her. Her hands stopped, but her agitation was still very evident.

"God, Suzy, I don't know how to do this." Her eyes flooded and she shook her head. "How did you get through it?"

"Honey, I didn't know in advance that I was going to lose Mark and Emma."

"No, I know, but — the time between when they fell off the boat to the time their bodies were found the next day. That had to be such torture."

Suzy gritted her teeth. She knew that, under normal circumstances, Rachel would never have brought up that time so obtusely.

Suzy never needed a reminder of that hideously dark day, since it was always there in her memory, but whenever she got one, it always brought it all back intensely. The waiting, the dread, the knowledge of what had happened, and the 99.9% certainty of the most likely outcome.

"Yeah," she sighed, "it was." She squeezed Rachel's shoulder and pulled her in for a hug. With that contact, the floodgates were opened and Rachel cried against Suzy's shoulder.

» § «

"There you are!" Suzy turned and saw Damien looking at her, his face not quite angry, but definitely strained. "Where were you?"

"I went to have lunch with Fin and Julie." Suzy frowned. "Is there a problem?"

"I—I just—" He sighed impatiently, his eyes casting wildly about the room. "I just didn't know where you went. I thought you were backing out or something."

Then, he shook his head.

"Of course, considering that nothing's really happening, if you wanted to back out, I think it would be fine."

"No, Damien, I gave you my word. I signed your contracts. You're getting your finale."

"Okay," he replied, his voice becoming a little less tense. "I just—I went looking for you and I didn't see you anywhere."

"You went looking for me?" Her frown deepened. "Did you go to the cottage?"

"Well, no, but I went out there on the path." His voice took on a bit more strength, a little less panic, and he sucked in a deep breath as he latched on to that explanation. "I mean I thought that's where you might have gone, but I didn't want to interrupt your time with your family. And you never came back."

Suzy narrowed her eyes as she looked at Damien, and she threw a quick glance at Rachel.

"Damien, I'm here now. I just came back around the other side of the house. I was looking at Shannon and Claire's playground."

"Oh," Damien replied, nodding his head. "Okay, that makes sense. I just—I wish you had let me know."

"Why, Damien? Is there anything wrong? Do you need me for something?"

"No," he said. His voice sounded tight, his vocal cords stretched to their limit. "No, sorry. I've just—I've never been this close to death before."

Suzy nodded understandingly. Damien looked squarely at her for a moment, then he sighed again. He turned and walked away, toward a group of people in the production company.

Suzy didn't understand the flash of anger she saw in that brief look he had given her.

¶uzy was only vaguely aware of James aiming his camera at her, but she was primarily focused on opening up her SpiritSense. She was anxious to find out if the banishment spell had worked.

She was dismayed when she felt herself being pulled into an episode.

» § «

"God, you're amazing!" Ron said as he rolled over, settling into the cool sheets. She smiled at the compliment. She felt that the same could be said of him.

She sometimes wondered how many had said it.

She snuggled up against Ron, her head on his left shoulder, but then she felt him jerk.

"Ow!" he said, his face wincing, and she remembered.

"Sorry," she said, pulling away and looking at his latest tattoo. "What is that again?" she asked.

"A heptagram," he replied. "It has supernatural significance in lots of different cultures."

"And why is it you want these?" she asked.

He quirked his lips at her comment, but he was patient with her.

"It's an artistic expression of something that's important to me," he replied.

"Hmm," she replied, settling her head more on his chest. At least that was still clear of markings. "How far are you planning on taking it?"

"I don't know," he replied, lifting his head to look at her. "Do you not like it?"

"You have such a beautiful body. It just seems a shame to mark it up like this."

"It's a form of self-expression," Ron said, "it's meaningful, and I think tattoos are sexy."

"Okay," she said noncommittally. "I think you're sexy, with or without them."

"Good answer," he smiled.

"But I thought I was the spirit medium of the family," she said playfully.

"The more experienced, perhaps," Ron conceded, "but I'm getting there."

"Yes, you are," she granted, and she stretched up to kiss him. Then, she swung her legs around and got out of bed.

"Where are you going?" Ron asked. He watched her as she gathered up her discarded clothing and began pulling it back on, stretching the shirt down over her belly.

"Shannon will be waking up from her nap soon. I'm going to go downstairs and get started on lunch."

"Okay, Kate," Ron replied. "I'll be downstairs in a few minutes."

» § «

Shannon, her dark hair bouncing in a short pageboy cut, giggled at Kate as she took another bite of her grilled cheese sandwich. Kate giggled back at her, making another face at the little girl.

Ron sat nearby, ignoring them.

"This is good," he finally said. Kate looked up at him, a little disoriented from suddenly being pulled from her goofiness with Shannon.

She looked at the papers in his hand.

"Yeah?" she asked.

"Absolutely. I remember after you produced several episodes of those ghost hunter shows, and even a Paranormal Activity movie, you always said you could do better." He held the papers up and shook them. "You're damn right. This looks really good!"

Kate glanced at Shannon, but she wasn't paying any attention to Ron. Like most parents, she didn't want her five-year-old adding curse words to her vocabulary just yet.

"Thank you."

"Yeah, babe, this is a great idea. Queen of the Dead." He looked up at her and smiled. "I guess that would make me King of the Dead, huh?"

Kate frowned and chuckled.

"Well, no more than being married to Elizabeth makes Prince Philip the king of England."

"Wait," Ron sat up straight and looked squarely at her, "you mean you don't want me to be a part of this show?"

"Of course you'll be part of it. But it's my show. You'll definitely be my right-hand man, but you're not going to have equal billing."

"I thought we were a team," Ron said testily.

"We are," Kate replied, her tone beginning to match his. She glanced at Shannon, then tilted her head out the door to the kitchen. Ron followed her.

"We're a team," Kate continued, "but that doesn't mean that everything's equal. In this case, assuming they buy the show, I'll be the quarterback. But we can't have two quarterbacks on the field. You'll be my running back, and together, we're going to score big!"

Ron looked at her for a few moments.

"Well, I guess that's better than nothing."

"It's a lot better than nothing. You'll play a big part in the production. But you won't be the one making the executive decisions. That'll be my job, the creator of the show."

Ron still looked a little annoyed.

"Honey," Kate continued, "I've had a connection to the spirit world for almost my whole life, ever since Gramma made contact with me when I was five. You know this. It's practically second nature to me."

"I know," Ron sighed.

"You've only been doing this for a few years."

"And you've said I'm getting really good."

"Yes. While I've always believed that someone either has the gift or they don't, your dedication to learning and applying yourself is convincing me that, even if someone doesn't initially have the ability, they can acquire it if it's something they really want.

"Though, as I've said before, I don't agree with your methods."

"My methods are effective," Ron replied impatiently.

"But I don't think they're very humane."

"Oh my god, Kate, we've been through this before. They're dead."

"Yes, but they're still sentient entities," Kate insisted. "They're individuals who are probably sad or confused as to why they're still here, or why the people they love won't interact with them.

"And then you use your magic spell book to conjure one into your presence, then use another spell to evict it. It just seems heartless to me. And potentially not even applicable to real-life situations."

"What are you talking about? I conjure and expel. It's like I have even more power."

"Exactly. What if conjuring a ghost gives you more power over it to begin with?"

"How is that a problem?" Ron demanded.

"What makes you think you'll have the same kind of power over a ghost we encounter in the wild, in a haunted house, or whatever we come across in the show? If you aren't the one who brought it into your presence, how do you know you'll have any power over expelling it?"

He glared at her.

"Well, I guess we'll just have to wait and see."

"Yes, we will."

Kate returned his glare. She was glad when Shannon called to her from the dining room.

» § «

The episode ended and Suzy sat there unmoving. She was confused and surprised. She hadn't wanted to be pulled into an episode with a demon, but now that she found it wasn't a demon after all, she was intrigued.

She was happy to see that nobody was around. She could hear voices in the room behind her, but nobody was nearby watching her. One of the bigger cameras was still aimed at her, and she could see that the red light indicated that it was recording, but nobody was behind it.

She decided to stay where she was and go into another episode.

27

Kate lay in the hospital bed holding Claire. The baby arrived without much fuss on a Friday evening. Kate looked lovingly down at the little round face. Shannon had Ron's dark hair, and now Claire had blonde hair like her own. Claire was sleeping peacefully in her arms, and Kate smiled as she gazed at her.

She raised her eyes to the chair beside the bed, the one where Ron would be sitting if he had been around for the birth of his daughter, and her smile faded. She had tried calling him when she felt the first contraction, but the call went straight to voicemail.

He had been gone for a good portion of the day, doing research and an interview for a story he was writing. As a freelance journalist, he was sometimes called away to work at inconvenient times.

He usually didn't turn his phone off, though. He might silence it if he was doing an interview, but her calls wouldn't go straight to voicemail.

When she couldn't contact him, Kate left a message and then called Gloria, a friend who lived a mile away. Jenny, Gloria's thirteen-year-old daughter stayed with Shannon while Gloria helped Kate through the delivery.

That had been a couple of hours ago, and still no word from Ron. Now, Gloria had gone home, and taken Shannon with her.

"Hey, baby."

Kate looked up toward the door as Ron rushed into the room.

"Hey." She watched him as he rounded the bed and zeroed in on the baby. "Where've you been?"

Ron looked up at Kate, looking a little startled.

"Oh, honey, I'm sorry. I was doing that interview. You knew that. But my battery died. I plugged my phone in in my car and left it charging while I did the interview. I didn't get your message until after it was done. I'm so sorry I wasn't here."

His apology was so sincere, and his reason made perfect sense. Kate felt bad about her accusatory tone. She shifted a little so that Ron could look at his daughter, and her suspicion vanished when she looked back down at the baby.

"She's beautiful, just like you," Ron said. "And she has your golden hair." He looked up at Kate. "Aw, honey, you done good. Really good!"

Kate looked at him, and seeing the consummate joy on his face, she regretted her earlier feelings of suspicion. She shifted Claire in her arms to position her so that Ron could hold her. As he carefully took her, Kate saw tears in his eyes.

» § «

"Honey, what – "

"Shh!" Kate cut him off when the baby jumped in her arms. She had been nursing Claire for ten minutes, and she was nearly asleep, until Ron walked in the room and spoke.

"Sorry," he said, lowering his voice. "What do you think about the name Damien Specter?"

"For what?" Kate whispered, annoyed.

"For me."

Kate looked up at him and frowned.

"You thinking of changing your name?"

"I am, and I think Damien Specter would be perfect for a ghost hunter."

As Claire's eyes had closed again, and stayed closed, Kate carefully popped the baby's mouth off her nipple, stood up and laid her down in her crib. She pulled the blanket up over her and ushered Ron out the door, refastening the flap of her nursing bra.

"You're really throwing yourself into this, aren't you?" she asked in her normal voice.

"Sure, why shouldn't I?" Ron replied. "I think it's important to create a persona."

"Will I need to change my name to Morgana Specter?" she asked sarcastically.

"No," Ron said hesitantly, "but that really does sound pretty cool."

"I'm not changing my name," she asserted, irritated that he didn't catch her satirical tone. "Are you forgetting all the bullshit I had to go through after we got married and I changed my last name to Herbert?"

"That's fine," Ron said dismissively. "Do what you want."

"Oh, well, thank you."

She chided herself for the sharp, sarcastic tone she used. It had been happening pretty frequently lately.

"Have you pitched your show concept yet?" Ron asked, apparently oblivious to Kate's irritation.

"No, sorry, I've been busy gestating, delivering and caring for our children."

She sighed as she realized that she did it again.

"Honey, you know how slowly networks move. You really need to get that rolling."

"Well, I can't really see myself doing a ghost-hunting show with a baby strapped to my back and a five-year-old's sticky hand stuck to mine, so . . ."

Shit.

28

Damien withdrew from the studio, holding his head. He headed toward the back of the house, to the family room. Rachel followed close behind.

"What is it, honey?" she asked, then she felt stupid. It was obvious what the problem was. He had a headache from the damn tumor that was killing him. Damien turned and looked as if he was surprised to see her.

"Oh, I didn't hear you," he said. Rachel thought he seemed irritated. "The headache's back."

"What can I get you?" she asked, hoping to stem the feeling of helplessness.

"Nothing," he said. He headed toward the liquor cabinet. He poured two fingers of Scotch into a glass and swallowed it down.

"Are you sure that's a good idea?" Rachel asked.

Damien looked at her and smirked.

"I'm going to be dead in a few hours," he said. He didn't seem to notice Rachel flinch. "Are you thinking I should have my wits about me?"

"I just don't know if it might make your headache worse."

"Alcohol is a depressant," he replied, a harsh tone in his voice, "so it has a calming effect. It's also an analgesic, so it helps to numb pain." He splashed more into the glass and held it up. "If this doesn't do it, then the goddamn suicide cocktail should do the trick."

He threw the drink back and sighed. He poured more into the glass and carried it, with the bottle, to his favorite chair and sat down.

"What the fuck is it with your friend, Suzy?" he asked.

Rachel frowned and sat down on the sofa near him.

"What? What are you talking about?"

"It's like she's got a death wish," he replied, taking another drink. When he realized what he said, he laughed. "Says the guy who's about to kill himself on TV."

He took a breath and got serious again.

"She's insisting on connecting with this demon. She's doing these fucking episodes, and I can't seem to break her free of them."

"Wait," Rachel said, "you've tried to break her connection?"

"Hell, yeah," Damien replied, draining the last of the whisky. He looked at Rachel and grinned. "Hold on, what am I worried about? I'll be dead and gone. I won't have any liability."

He poured more whisky into the glass, then stopped, frowning as if it was becoming more difficult to think. It took a few seconds for the pain to pass enough that he could utter a coherent sentence.

"I *am* concerned about my girls, though. I don't want to leave any darkness over them, whether it's this demon, or the death — or worse — of a self-destructive ghost hunter. Or the knowledge of any culpability of their father."

Rachel looked at him from under lowered brows.

"What culpability?"

Damien looked up, surprised again that he wasn't just speaking to himself. He motioned in the direction of his studio, spilling some of the Scotch on Rachel.

"Whatever happens to Suzy while she's connected to this demon, she's in my home. That'll leave a shroud over this house that my girls will have to live with. It'll also leave a stain on the memory that my girls, and my fans, will have of me. I want to be remembered in a good light, not as some kind of monster."

"Look," Rachel replied, wiping the whisky off her arm and onto her jeans, struggling to keep her voice even, "I know Suzy. She's thorough and she's careful. She's not going to endanger herself unnecessarily. And she'll very likely have a very interesting story to tell when she's done."

Damien gazed at her through bleary eyes. He looked down at his glass, studying it as if trying to decide what to do with it.

Rachel hadn't expected him to look worried about her response.

Damien sighed and drank down the whisky.

29

Kate came in and put down her purse and the folder. She tilted her head in a couple of directions but couldn't hear anything. That wasn't unusual in such a large structure, but with a seven-year-old and a two-year-old in the house, she could usually get a hint.

She headed toward the back of the castle, to the family room. She had seen James' car when she drove up, so she figured she'd start there.

"Hey, babe," Ron said when she walked in. Her instincts had been right. James and Ron were both there, a bottle of beer beside each of them.

She leaned over and gave Ron a quick kiss, then smiled at James.

"Where are the girls?" she asked Ron.

"Shannon's playing in the playroom and Claire's napping."

Seeing the baby monitor on the coffee table, she nodded, satisfied.

"So?" Ron asked. "What did they say?"

"They liked it," Kate replied, nodding.

Two TV executives that Kate knew personally had a couple of meetings on the east coast and, at her request, had added an additional stop in Bangor so she could pitch her idea for **Queen of the Dead**.

"Yeah?" Ron, becoming visibly excited, rose from his chair and pulled Kate into his arms.

"Congratulations, Kate," James said.

"Well, thank you," Kate replied, trying to keep the conversation grounded, and not buying into the excitement. "But it's not a done deal yet."

"No, but it's finally on the way," Ron said. "And we already have a boots-on-the-ground cameraman."

"What?" Kate asked, pulling away from Ron.

"James is onboard. He said he'd love to do it."

Kate looked at James, then back at Ron. She took a shaky breath, struggling to keep her anger in check. It was becoming more and more difficult lately, but she was determined to not fight in front of James.

"I'm sorry, James," she said, glancing at him, but her eyes were immediately drawn back to her husband. "Ron shouldn't have said anything about this yet. And he certainly should not have been offering anybody positions in the show."

"Come on, Kate," Ron protested, "it's a great idea. I was confident."

"It doesn't matter. It's a bare bones idea in its extremely early stages. There isn't even funding for a pilot yet."

"But babe – "

"And even more than that," Kate interrupted, her tone colder, and with an apologetic glance at James, "if it gets off the ground, it will be my show. It is not your place to be lining up the cast and crew."

Ron took a step back as if Kate had hit him. James uncomfortably cleared his throat and lifted his beer bottle. He drained it, then stood up.

"Maybe I should be going," he said quietly.

Ron looked at him, then looked back at Kate, an accusing expression on his face.

"Sorry, James," he said.

Kate and Ron stood there glaring at each other until they heard the distant sound of the front door.

"How dare you," Ron said. "James is my oldest and dearest friend. You had no right to treat him like that."

"I didn't treat James badly, nor am I the one who put him in that position in the first place." Kate's voice dropped even lower and colder as her anger came to the fore. "You had no right to interfere with my show, so how dare you!"

Ron was about to fire back a response when they heard sounds from the baby monitor. Without another look at Ron, Kate turned and headed up toward the nursery.

» § «

She would have to go back to work. Not something that she had to physically be in Hollywood for. Not yet. She couldn't leave her girls for extended periods. Years ago, before she started producing and directing, she had been a screenwriter. She could do that again. It was something that she could do from wherever she was, in the comfort of her own home.

Wherever that ended up being.

Then, if Queen of the Dead *takes off, she could look for hauntings nearby to start with. Maine was full of places purported to be haunted.*

But something had to change.

She looked at the pair of jeans again. They had been enough to get her to stop loading the washing machine.

Ron, or Damien, as he was insisting on being called now, had talked about hiring a live-in nanny or au pair, *or even just a part-time maid, someone to take some of the household burden off of Kate's shoulders. Someone to watch the girls, cook meals, do cleaning and laundry.*

But Kate didn't consider it a burden. It was her responsibility, yes, but not a burden. She was happy to do it for her girls. It was her job, but one she loved.

Damien, though, well, she was finding him to be a different story. He was becoming a burden.

Nearly every day, he had a new idea for Queen of the Dead. *That, in itself, wasn't a problem. She had always welcomed input from others about her shows.*

But Damien seemed almost as if he was trying to take it over. He wanted a bigger part in it, and more control of its content. He wanted to research and deliver historical background for their cases. He wanted to set the mood with what he called "eloquent narration."

Admittedly, some of his ideas weren't bad. But when he suggested something that she didn't like, that she didn't think went well with her concept of the show, he became angry, offended. As if she were personally insulting or attacking him.

The show hadn't even been picked up yet. She had only recently been told that she had approval to create a pilot. And already Ron – Damien was a pain in the ass.

Then, she found the jeans.

She had been sorting loads. Darks were on the right, lights on the left. There was a pair of Shannon's blue jeans. They were faded, but still she put them in the pile on the right. Same with the navy overalls that Claire seemed to love.

Then, Damien's black jeans.

It wouldn't have even been an issue if it hadn't been for the coincidental timing of the music. She had Pandora pumping out a playlist that she liked, and "Counting Stars" by OneRepublic had just ended. "Come With Me Now" by KONGOS had not started yet. In that brief space between songs, she heard it.

As she was putting Damien's jeans in the right pile, she heard a light crinkling sound. She pulled them back and felt around. She pulled out a receipt. It had been wadded up and hastily stashed in the front pocket.

The Lucky-U Motel was a dumpy little motel on the west side of Bangor. It was not uncommon for Damien to check in to a hotel when he had to travel for a story he was working on.

But in Bangor, at 1:34 on a Friday afternoon, there was only one thing that came to mind. Something that Kate had already been suspicious of for quite a while.

She sighed, wondering where she was going to end up.

What the hell am I thinking, she suddenly thought to herself. This is *my* house. I'm not going anywhere.

30

Kate closed the door to Claire's room and walked down the hall. She quietly cracked open the door to Shannon's room and peeked in. In the glow of the Elsa night light, she could see that the girl was obviously asleep, a few strands of her dark hair draped over her eyes, and fluttering with each breath. Kate resisted the urge to go in and brush the hair away.

She eased the door closed. After several seconds, when she felt an ache, she realized that she was still gripping the door handle. She let go of it and flexed her fingers several times. She pulled in a deep breath and blew it out as a shaky exhalation.

She was surprised at how much resolve it required to turn and head toward the stairs at the end of the hall. As she took one step after another, she looked at the torch sconces with the flickering flame bulbs that lined the hall. She remembered the antique bronze lantern-style sconces that she had wanted.

She looked up at the architectural details, the dark, rough-hewn timbers that crossed the ceiling throughout the house. She remembered the warm honey-colored oak that she had wanted.

At the end of the hall, she glanced out the window. The blackness outside seemed to match her mood, especially when she regarded the dark scarlet velvet drapery that framed the window. She remembered the soft ivory sheers that she had wanted.

She had envisioned a light, fairy-tale castle. But by the time the structure was finished, Shannon was two years old and a major handful. Ron took over decorating duties, and Kate was too tired to argue. In fact, she remembered feeling relief at the time.

By the time it was completed, though, her happily ever after Cinderella castle had been turned into a set from Game of Thrones, Ron's favorite new show. It resulted in a lot of fights, with Ron justifying his choices, occasionally apologizing, but that was usually, she knew, just to get Kate off his ass. In most cases, it was too late to change without incurring a great deal more expense, so she just sighed and let it go.

She hadn't realized until now how long-lasting her resentment had been. She missed what she had originally planned for her home. She had accepted several of Ron's suggestions and requests all through the project, the project that she paid for. She had wanted a sparkling white design like the castle in Disneyland, or the Neuschwanstein Castle in Germany, one of its inspirations. Ron had suggested that a grey granite-looking structure might be better, more authentic. Kate had allowed it.

Other suggestions for alterations had come, and some, she had allowed, while others she had denied. By the time it was finished, though, her light and airy fairy-tale retreat had become a dark and menacing stronghold.

After they had been living in the place for nearly a year, Ron had suggested that she see a doctor about the dark moods she was experiencing. She did, and he prescribed an antidepressant, which gave limited results.

Now, she couldn't believe how extensive Ron's control issues were, and how she hadn't recognized them until now. His recent attempts to hijack her show had been presaged by numerous red flags throughout the years.

At the bottom of the stairs, she turned toward the family room. Ron was sitting in his favorite chair, sipping a glass of Scotch and reading. Kate took a deep breath and forced her feet to keep carrying her forward.

"Ron, I – "

"Damien," he interrupted without looking up from his book. "It's official, remember?"

Kate sighed and sat down on the sofa.

"Damien, I need to talk to you."

He read for a few more seconds, then placed his fingertip on the page to mark his place. He looked up expectantly at Kate. A few more seconds passed.

"I want a divorce," she finally said.

It took several seconds for the words to register in his brain. When they finally did, Damien frowned. He closed his book, not bothering to mark the page, and put it down on the dark rough-hewn coffee table in front of him.

"You – " He didn't finish and left the word hanging there.

"I want a divorce," Kate repeated.

Damien looked away from her for a moment, but if anything, his frown deepened. He pulled his gaze back to her.

"Kate, what the fuck?"

"I've had it with your control issues – "

"What control issues?" he interrupted again, his voice rising.

Kate closed her eyes, gathering strength, forcing herself to remain calm. She remembered all of her thoughts in the hallway since she put Claire to bed. God, was that only five minutes ago? It seemed like hours.

When she opened her eyes again, she kept them pointed down toward the floor, away from Damien's intimidating gaze.

"You have seized control of so much of my life. This house, for example, is almost nothing like what I wanted before you took over the decorating duties, without asking me, I might add. And as I think about it now, I can remember other instances before and since where you've done the same thing."

"Oh my god, Kate. If you have a problem with something I do or say, talk to me about it. Don't just give me an ultimatum."

"I'm not giving you an ultimatum. You don't have to change if you don't want to. I want a divorce. That's all."

"Well, shit. Why is this the first I'm even hearing about this?"

"It's not, Ron," Kate lifted her eyes up to his. He didn't bother to correct the name. "Don't you remember all the fights we had when you kept changing the décor from what I wanted to what you wanted?"

He looked away again and shook his head in frustration.

"God damn it, Kate," he looked back at her. "You want a divorce because I have different tastes in décor than you do?"

"It's not that we have different taste," she sighed. "It's that you don't think that my wishes are important enough to even consider. What you want is all that matters."

Damien's eyes bored into her. As she looked back at him, she drew strength from the other issue.

"But that's not the only reason I want a divorce," she said, pulling the once crumpled receipt from her pocket. "I've also had it with your infidelity."

Damien grimaced until he focused on the Lucky U logo at the top. He opened his mouth, but when nothing came out after a couple of seconds, Kate spoke up again.

"I don't want to hear explanations or excuses. I know this isn't a one-time thing. I've suspected it for a long time, and I'm done."

Damien looked away again, gathering his thoughts.

"This is going to make working on our show pretty awkward," he said in a grim tone of voice.

"Ron, it's not our show. It's *my* show, and I don't want you working on it." His head snapped back around. Kate continued. "I'm sorry. I know you wanted to get out of journalism and do something in front of the camera. I know you were hoping this was going to be your means for doing that, but you're going to have to find another way to get your foot in the door."

The desperation she saw on his face at that statement outstripped the expressions she had seen up until then.

» § «

Kate thought that giving Damien a month to find a place to live and clear his things out of the castle was pretty generous. She knew that Bangor was not a big city, so housing options were more limited than they would be in Boston or New York or Los Angeles.

Also, considering his desire to achieve stardom on screen, a month might allow him time to find a place to live in Hollywood, if that was the direction he wanted to go.

She had insisted that he move out of their bedroom immediately, though, so he had moved into a guest room. He hadn't been happy about it, but apparently, he hadn't seen any way around it.

Still, she was a little surprised when, after several days had passed, he was still around. Obviously, she didn't expect him to have moved out by then but, by outward appearances, he didn't seem to be making any effort toward finding a new place to live. He was always at home, never venturing out. But, of course, she didn't know what attempts he had made. He could have sent email *inquiries and phone messages and just been waiting to hear back. And since she had given him a month, she didn't say anything.*

She wasn't sure what to say, shortly after that, when she was getting ready to drive into town for groceries. Loading the girls into her car, she saw a pentagram carved into the workbench that Ron — Damien — sometimes used in the garage. She knew of his growing interest in the occult, so it wasn't a huge surprise. But she didn't understand the melted black wax on the points of the star, or the burn marks in the middle of it.

Then, there was the rock, the deep black stone coated with wax, apparently from the candles, with her name scraped into the wax.

She seldom paid any attention to what he was doing on the work bench, though. It was only the fact that she was looking for evidence that he was making moves toward getting out that she even looked at it. This could have been from any of a number of old projects that Damien had worked on ages ago.

She shook her head and climbed into her car.

amien sat hunched at the work bench in his garage. In front of him burned five black candles arranged in a circle, at the five points of the star gouged into the surface of the bench. In the center stood a miniature cauldron identical to the one on the altar in his studio.

He ground a few leaves of henbane with his mortar and pestle, and tipped the resulting powder into the cauldron. He hurriedly mixed the ingredients, while trying not to leave out anything, or change up the order. That was extremely important. Everything had to be exactly right.

He wished he hadn't been so weak a few minutes earlier. He never got drunk, never lost control. He knew that, given the timing and the circumstances, nobody would blame him. He was under more stress than he had endured in years. Still, that weakness could cost him. And Rachel had witnessed it. She hadn't been happy when he sent her away, back to the studio, but she went.

Now, his head was buzzing from the alcohol, so he had to be especially careful, and purge all other thoughts from his mind. He looked at the page again, squinting as he tried to focus and concentrate. The blood was next.

He picked up the X-Acto knife and poked the point into his thumb. He allowed a few drops of blood to drip into the mixture. After that, he held his thumb over a small cup and squeezed, forcing several drops into it, then stuck his thumb in his mouth to stem the bleeding.

He idly wondered how much alcohol was in his blood right now, and if that would affect the outcome.

He couldn't figure out why the banishment spell hadn't worked.

Either time!

Granted, he didn't know if a banishment spell was supposed to work on an already bound entity, but still, after being unbound, why hadn't the second one worked? He was intimately familiar with the spell, but still he had looked over it, examining each step, and he knew he had done everything correctly. If only that had worked, he wouldn't have to be doing this one.

But then there wouldn't be much of a show, either. Not that it was a gripping narrative. There was virtually nothing happening!

Damien knew that there were many who looked with disdain on magical spells as a bunch of superstitious nonsense, at best. And he knew as well as anyone that it wasn't an exact science. But still, by all outward appearances, the binding spell seemed to have worked. Why didn't the banishment spell?

He shook his head, then quickly closed his eyes when the movement induced a bout of dizziness. He took a deep breath and sighed. When the lightheadedness eased, he slowly opened his eyes, sighing with relief that the dizziness did not return.

He picked up the small piece of goat skin vellum and the quill fashioned from the wing feather of a crow. Damien had taken great pains to acquire the exact items specified in the spell in the grimoire, rather than making do with modern replicas.

He dipped the quill into the small puddle of blood that he had squeezed into the cup and scratched something on the vellum. Putting the quill aside, he held the vellum over the flame of the candle on the point of the star closest to him. Once it started to flame, he laid it on top of the mixture in the little cauldron.

He picked up the tarnished silver spoon lying to the side of the pentagram and used it to stir the contents of the cauldron, counterclockwise, mixing it thoroughly. He leaned back, careful to not inhale the smoke of the dry henbane that sparked and caught fire.

Damien looked at everything arranged on the table in front of him, comparing it with the instructions in the grimoire. The black stone coated with fresh wax was there, a new name now engraved in the wax.

All five candles were burning steadily, while the contents of the cauldron were smoldering.

He nodded and looked at the grimoire again, reading the words directly from the page. There was no room for error as he spoke the ancient spell over the cauldron, following the pronunciation guides he had added.

Aignau yashya naam dashami saa vinyashyati.
Tashyah jivahnam saada nishprabham bravishyati.

He pulled his eyes away from the words on the page and looked at the mixture in the cauldron. It was little more than ash, now.

Satisfied that everything had been done correctly, he blew out the candles, starting with the one directly in front of him, and moving counterclockwise.

As five tendrils of smoke wound their way upward, he sat back and heaved a heavy sigh. He looked at his watch. He would go check in a few minutes.

hy am I here?" Doctor Taylor demanded.

The little room with the hard chairs and the table and the requisite mirror on the wall to the side were intimidating, but he tried to keep up the bluster.

The man sitting opposite him, Detective Adams, raised his eyebrows in an expression that indicated disbelief.

"We have it on record that you were informed of the charges when you were arrested."

"Remind me," Taylor insisted.

Adams sighed and opened the folder in front of him.

"Medical negligence, malpractice and insurance fraud. There are also some drug charges here. It seems you weren't satisfied just with fucking up your patients."

He closed the folder and looked back up at Taylor.

Doctor Taylor thought that allowing a few seconds, hearing the charges again, might help him know what to say, how to respond to the accusations.

He sighed when he realized that he was wrong.

"Who's charging me with this?"

Adams snickered.

"The District Attorney."

"I mean, who's my accuser? Who have I supposedly defrauded? Who has been the alleged victim of malpractice?"

Adams sighed and opened the folder again. He lifted a page and started reading names.

"Emily Jorgensen, Walter Buchanan, Jeremy Munson, Damien Specter, JoAnn —"

"Damien Specter!" Taylor exclaimed, jabbing a finger toward Adams. He sat up straighter, his eyes open wide, his face tensed with excitement.

Adams shook his head and sat back. It seemed as if it was going to be a long night.

» § «

"That son of a bitch!" Doctor Sun grumbled as he pushed aside a patient's folder and pulled another folder in front of him. A few other doctors gathered around the conference table looked up at him, but nobody replied. They went back to their own folders.

Sun opened the folder and began reading the patient's record. He looked at the first entry, from the patient's first visit.

"Patient complains of intense headaches. Affects his balance, ability to focus on responsibilities, ability to move and perform normal tasks."

Sun scanned through the doctor's notes concerning follow-up exams. Numerous tests were performed, including a brain MRI.

The doctor's diagnosis was glioblastoma. Sun flipped through the other pages of the file and frowned.

The film was included with the folder, and Sun held it up to the light. The white mass was very clearly visible on the scan.

Sun put the film down on the table and turned back to the folder, but something drew his attention back to the MRI. He frowned, trying to determine what it was that had caught his attention.

Then, he saw it. The label on the lower corner of the film. The radiologist had scribbled the pertinent information on it, including the date.

Sun looked back at the record in the folder, and he frowned.

"Does anyone have a patient with brain tumor symptoms, and an MRI ordered on June 9th?"

The other doctors looked up at him, shaking their heads.

"Wait."

Sun looked at Joyce Whittier, neurologist. She leaned forward, shuffling through a few other folders in front of her. She opened one and glanced into it, shook her head and pushed it aside. The next one, she opened, then she picked it up.

"Yes. Marjorie Fenwick, 49. Complained of severe headaches and dizziness. An MRI was ordered on June 9th, but came back clear. Ibuprofen was recommended for milder headaches, and sumatriptan was prescribed for the more severe."

"When was the MRI performed?" Sun asked.

Joyce looked back down at the file.

"June 9th."

"Do you have the film?"

"Yes," she replied, holding it up. It was clear.

"What's the date on the label?" Sun asked.

Joyce looked at it and frowned.

"June 7th."

Sun slapped the file in front of him.

"That son of a bitch. He ordered this MRI on June 7th. He mixed up the films and fucked up their diagnoses."

He pulled out his cell phone and looked at the patient information on the file in front of him.

"You better call Marjorie," he said to Joyce, "and get her in here right away!"

The call was already ringing as Sun put the phone against his ear. It rang once before being sent to voice mail. He disconnected and tried again, with the same result. Sighing, he left a message this time, leaving his own number.

He touched the disconnect button and looked up at Joyce as she quietly said goodbye. She looked stricken as she disconnected from her call.

"Marjorie Fenwick died two weeks ago," she said.

"That son of a bitch!" Sun said.

He looked back down at the file in front of him, scanning through the remaining lines.

Suddenly, he sat forward, his eyes widening as he read the prognosis and treatment information.

"Oh my god!"

He jumped up and ran out of the conference room, leaving the other doctors looking at each other before turning their attention back to their collective files.

What's this, Damien?" Kate asked. She looked at the plate with the chips and sandwich that Damien held out to her. "What's going on?"

"It's just a peace offering," Damien replied. "It's your favorite, garden veggies and hummus on sourdough."

Kate looked suspiciously at him as she took the plate.

"I know I haven't exactly been easy to live with," Damien added.

"No, you haven't. But we've already been through that."

"I know, and I promise this isn't a lame attempt to weasel my way back." He looked askance at her. "Although, if you were willing to give it another go, I wouldn't be averse to it."

Kate returned the look as she took a bite of the sandwich.

"Why are you still here?"

"Why, is my time up?" Damien replied innocently. Kate narrowed her eyelids but tried not to show her irritation.

"It's been almost four weeks. Next Monday is a month, so yes, your time is almost up. You haven't told me about any of your efforts to find another place to live."

"Well, I didn't think you were that interested in talking to me anymore. But I assure you, Kate, I have been busy making plans. You have nothing to worry about."

Damien had first made this sandwich for her a few years ago, piled high with things like grated carrots and roasted red peppers and sun-dried tomatoes and avocado. She had raved about it and begged him to make it for her on a regular basis.

He agreed, although now that she thought about it, it seemed as if he only made it for her when he had screwed up somehow. She realized that, too many times, with the sandwich in her belly, there had been too many instances in which she had relented and forgiven him for whatever offense he had committed.

Not this time!

» § «

She was so sleepy! It must be the stress she had been going through lately, with Damien. She hadn't been sleeping well. She had never thought that their relationship would end up this way. They had been so in love!

Too many love stories she knew of had ended in tragedy. But her parents had remained together for all these years, and Kate had been determined from the start that she and Damien would be the same.

Unfortunately, the success of a relationship was dependent on more than just one person.

Her nerves had been on edge for weeks now, and her sleep had been sporadic and fleeting. It's no wonder she was so tired.

She closed her eyes for just an instant, although when she opened them again, she was surprised to find that she was in bed. She didn't remember moving to the bedroom.

Damien was there and, despite her fuzzy vision, she saw him place a little orange plastic bottle on her nightstand.

"Hey, babe," he said when he saw her looking at him. "Here, this will help you feel better."

He lifted her head, his other hand up against her mouth.

Her thoughts were muddled. Damien was — what? She felt like there was something she should remember about Damien, but all she could think about was their first date, and how he had made her feel like such a princess. He loved her so much!

And now he wanted to help her to feel better.

She opened her mouth. She barely even noticed the pills on her tongue before he tipped a glass of water against her lips. As the water flowed into her mouth, she closed her eyes and her mouth and swallowed, glad that she would feel better soon.

She was so sleepy. She'd just close her eyes for a bit, and when she woke up, she'd feel so much better!

God bless Damien!

» § «

She couldn't believe the level of anger she felt! And she was barely able to even process the fact that she was looking down on her own body. How could that be? Seeing her own body from a vantage point a few feet above her?

Her body was lying there on her bed, still wearing the clothes that she had been wearing as she ate the sandwich that Damien had brought her.

She bunched her eyebrows together, but she noticed that her eyebrows (in front of her!) didn't move.

There, on the nightstand beside her body, was a prescription bottle, and a note. The note was in a handwriting that was strikingly similar to her own.

I'm so sorry, Damien. It's too hard. I just can't do it anymore. Please take care of our girls!

That fucking bastard! She could see in an instant what he had done. He had likely ground up two or three sleeping pills into the hummus to make her sleepy, then gave her the rest of them afterwards. That realization, obvious as it was, seemed so surreal as she thought about it.

She was dead?

amien was wound up tight. He had never been so tense in his life!

Suzy was *still* there, *still* in the same position that he had seen her in the last time he was in the studio. She had been right. Her SpiritSensor activities made for *really* fucking boring TV!

Still, he was concerned about what she might be learning, assuming her crazy description of what she did was accurate. Was it possible that she could really be communicating with Kate?

But Kate was so out of it at the end, barely awake at all, even when he gave her the additional pills. Would she even be able to put together what had happened to her?

The fact that her ghost had been so hostile toward him after her death did tend to lead him to the conclusion that she had somehow figured it out.

He looked closely for a few moments and saw that Suzy was still breathing.

Shit!

So, the death spell didn't work on her any better than it had on Kate. He idly wondered if the binding spell would work on a living human.

He also wondered if he could somehow get sleeping pills into Suzy.

God, why did I ever get Suzy involved in this?

Of course, he knew why.

First of all, his ratings had been sliding lately. It was looking as if three seasons were all he was going to get, even without the brain tumor. His vanity, though, made him want to go out with a bang. He was pretty certain that on-air suicide would likely do that. Viewers loved a good, dark twist.

But a final episode team-up with the SpiritSensors would definitely solidify it. He had been honest about that. Crossovers were cool. Especially crossovers that looked as good as Suzy. Rachel was pretty, and a good lay, but damn! That Suzy was hot stuff!

Also, there was the fact that he hadn't really understood what it was that she did. Even after she described it to him, in their kitchen, he had a hard time believing that she truly connected with the ghosts as she said she did. Channeling them? Living their lives? Seeing what they saw? How could anyone do that? He almost thought that she was as much of a fake as he was.

He had to admit that he had begun thinking that they were as much of a fraud as they had accused him of being.

But there was also the other shit that he realized had influenced him to some extent. The religious dogma that had remained lodged in his mind. Having Christian doctrine hammered into his head at Precious Blood Catholic School, followed by a few years at Ben Hillel Academy after his mother converted to Judaism, had done a number on him.

He was already convinced that there was an afterlife. He had made a tidy living off of it in the last few years.

But what if there really was a heaven as the Christians are so convinced of, or a *Gan Eden* as many Jews believe? Had he fucked up his chances of getting a good judgment by killing his wife?

If that final judgment was a real thing, he knew that was a silly question. He was already pretty much screwed.

And now, having learned that Suzy's schtick might actually be real, here he was trying to kill her, as well. But as bothersome as those afterlife questions were, the *current* life issues were *at least* as important to him.

He didn't want to leave this life being thought of as an unfaithful husband, a fraud and a murderer. He was soon going to be dead, but he wanted to leave behind a good, solid reputation. He didn't want people seeing him as a vile person.

He wanted immortality, if not in reality, then at least through his legacy.

And, for all his faults, he loved his girls, and he didn't want them to be seen as the offspring of a monster.

If there was any chance of leaving them a decent life, he had to prevent Suzy from knowing what had happened.

If only she hadn't been distracted by their swing set!

It hadn't been hot out there. It was November. But he had been sweating as he stood there with a rock in his hand waiting for Suzy to return to the studio after lunch. He had no idea how he would explain it to everybody after the deed was done. Maybe Fin had been possessed by the demon and killed her.

It was a stretch, but still, he had to protect his reputation.

But it didn't matter, since she hadn't returned that way. Then, he'd had to cover his tracks when he got angry at Suzy after she came back. He blamed the alcohol. He really had to get control of that. He didn't want to leave being seen as a lousy drunk, either.

He drew in a deep breath and blew it out. A glance at the camera trained on her chair told him that it was still recording. There was nothing he could do here and now.

He shook his head and looked around. He saw James, his camera on his shoulder, at the altar.

His face contorted into a frown as he went over to see what James was filming.

"What's up?" Damien asked, trying to pitch his voice normally.

James looked at him, and then back down at the altar.

"I don't know," James replied, his face expressing confusion. "People have been moving all around the studio. I don't think they're accustomed to being confined in a space for so long without any scripted activity taking place."

Damien looked down at the altar and saw what James had zeroed in on.

The candle had fallen over, and the flame had gone out. Maybe it had been knocked over by someone, or the table had just been bumped when a group of people had been conversing nearby. At any rate, it hadn't burned all the way down.

Facing up toward the camera, in the remainder of the candle that hadn't burned, what was left of what Damien had engraved was clearly visible.

Damien remembered when he was scraping it into the candle, wishing that James would go away. He had been more specific with this one. The "n" of the word "demon" was still visible, followed by "Kate."

» § «

"Ron, what's going on?" James asked.

"God dammit, my name's Damien!"

"Sorry." James pointed at the remains of the candle. "Kate?"

"It's nothing, James. Don't worry about it."

James sighed, frustrated.

"Is Kate the so-called demon you're trying to get rid of?"

Damien felt the ebbing stress he had felt a while back returning, along with the remaining effects of the Scotch, and he just felt so tired!

He put his head back and sighed, trying to think of how to respond.

Before he could, he heard the tone of the buzzer at the gates. Damien rolled his eyes, wondering who could be calling now.

He went over to the door of his studio where one of the receivers was located. He frowned at the image on the screen. He didn't recognize the man in the car waiting for a response.

He pressed the button and leaned toward the panel.

"Yes?"

"Hello," the man replied, "I'm Dr. Sun. I was a colleague of Dr. Taylor. I need to speak to Damien Specter immediately!"

Damien's frown deepened, but he pushed the button to open the gate. If nothing else, maybe speaking to this Dr. Sun would give him a few moments to think of how to respond to James. And to think of what to do about Suzy.

And Kate.

35

The episode was over, but Suzy was still in the chair, still psychically connected to Kate. In a few of her past send-offs, the ghost might actually appear in front of Suzy and talk with her before going on its way. But even though some of the production crew had wandered off, there were still several in the studio.

"I'm not prepared to show myself to a crowd," she told Suzy, "especially if it gets captured on camera and improves the ratings of Ronald's show."

Suzy smirked at Kate's use of Damien's given name.

"I'm sorry about the whole 'evil spirit' thing," Suzy said. "Damien insisted that it was a demon haunting his house."

"Yeah, I think he's almost started believing his narrative himself. He's certainly garnered plenty of sympathy for it."

"So, the binding spell worked, but the expulsion spell didn't," Suzy mused.

"The binding spell *didn't* work," Kate replied. "But he had started talking to James about getting a priest to perform an exorcism. I didn't know if that would work or not, and I didn't want to find out. So, I decided to cool it so I could stay here and watch over my girls."

"I don't blame you," Suzy said sympathetically. "I probably would have done the same thing."

"What happens now?" Kate asked, her face looking wary.

"That's entirely up to you," Suzy replied warmly. "I never try to force anyone to move on unless they're endangering someone else. But I do encourage it, simply because it will likely be a better existence than the one you have now."

"What about Ron?"

Suzy shook her head thoughtfully.

"I know the truth now. Realistically, though, I don't have any illusions that my psychic visions will be accepted by the authorities as valid evidence. But I promise I will try to clear the air about your death. It won't make any difference as far as Damien is concerned, since he'll be dying soon, but Claire and Shannon certainly deserve to know the truth about their mother."

Phantom tears filled Kate's eyes as she nodded and smiled.

» § «

"I'm not dying?" Damien asked, his face trying to decide whether to be happy, angry or hysterical.

"No," Dr. Sun replied, smiling, looking at all the people gathered behind Damien. "Dr. Taylor got your diagnosis mixed up with someone else's."

He was thinking *That son of a bitch!* again, but he managed to keep it to himself.

Damien just stood there stunned.

"I was going to administer the drugs in just a couple of hours."

"Oh, my god!" Dr, Sun replied breathlessly. "I'm glad I got here when I did."

Damien was dazed as he turned, looking at everyone in his foyer. James was there, too, the ubiquitous camera on his shoulder, recording the exchange. He could see the smile on James' face.

"But," Damien turned back to Dr. Sun, "Dr. Taylor showed me the film. I saw the big mass in my brain."

"That wasn't your brain. That was Marjorie Fenwick's."

"But what about my headaches?"

"Your symptoms point to a diagnosis of migraine. The diagnosis that was given to Marjorie Fenwick, whose film was mixed up with yours, and who, unfortunately, has since died from the tumor." Dr. Sun sighed. "Fortunately for you, migraines, well, they're unpleasant at times, but they're certainly not life-threatening. Based on what I saw in your file, I think you can expect to have a few more decades ahead of you."

Damien smiled, a little bewildered, as he turned toward the others again.

"Well," he said, a little flustered, "I guess we need to rethink the next episode."

Then, he remembered Suzy.

With the panic taking over, he suddenly turned and ran back toward his studio.

» § «

Suzy pushed herself up from the chair, fighting against the usual sluggishness that afflicted her when she came out of an episode. She looked around and was surprised to find that she was alone. The whole studio had cleared out, except for her.

The red light was still lit on the camera, so she knew that it had recorded her "sleeping" for however long she was in the episodes.

Suddenly, the door banged open and Damien ran into the room, straight toward her.

"What did you see?" he demanded, then more loudly. "What did you see?"

Suzy realized that it was too late to get her phone and call the police. She felt a little more comfortable, though, when she saw James following him in, his camera on his shoulder.

"I saw Kate," she replied. "I saw you kill her. I saw you grind up sleeping pills and put them in her sandwich to make her sleepy, then I saw you give her more sleeping pills to finish her off."

She knew she was stretching it a bit, since she hadn't actually seen him grind up the pills and put them in the hummus in the sandwich, but when she saw the panic in his

176

eyes, she knew her—and Kate's—assessment had been pretty accurate.

Still, she was a little surprised when he rushed her, gripping his hands around her neck. Under the weight of him, she fell back onto the floor, but he followed her down, his hands never leaving her throat.

Suzy was aware of a sharp bump on the back of her head as she hit the floor. She was aware of the painful pressure closing off her breath.

She wasn't aware of how long he had been choking her, though she was gasping and coughing and wheezing by the time James pulled Damien off of her.

She pushed herself up, sucking painful breaths down her throat. She was chagrined when she saw the camera carelessly tossed onto the loveseat when James had intervened on her behalf, though she was certainly grateful for his intervention.

Damien was sitting on the floor, still angrily struggling against James' hold of both his arms.

"Let me go, God dammit!" Damien shouted.

"Are you going to do anything stupid?" James asked.

"Wouldn't surprise me a bit," Damien replied.

Suzy almost laughed at his response, but the raspiness in her throat placed a bit of a hindrance on her current sense of humor.

James let go of his arms, but he pushed him back against the loveseat, holding him in place.

Suzy glanced up and saw Rachel looking at the three of them with her eyes wide. She didn't know how long she had been there, or how much she heard. But the look of horror on her face told Suzy that she had heard enough.

The tone sounded again from the panel near the door. Someone else was wanting in the front gate.

Damien started to lift himself up, but James pushed him back.

"Just stay there," he said. "They can wait."

Damien flashed an angry look at him, but the anger gradually transformed into something more like an exhausted indifference.

"Did you kill Kate?" James asked.

Damien sighed and leaned back against the loveseat, his head back.

"Suzy's crazy," he said. "She's even more of a fraud than we are. She's just making shit up."

"Did you kill her?" James repeated.

Damien looked at him, a look of disgust on his face.

"You're listening to the story of some goddam ghost whisperer? You think I would kill the love of my life?"

"I'm not going to ask you again," James said.

"Good!" Damien returned. "I'm getting pretty fucking sick of hearing it!"

"Damien Spector?"

They all turned toward the door and saw a man in a suit, accompanied by two uniformed police officers. The rest of the production crew were gathered there behind them.

Damien sighed.

hat can I do for you, Detective?" Damien asked after Detective Adams introduced himself. They were still standing in the studio area.

"We'd like for you to come downtown to answer some questions."

"About what?"

"About the murder of your wife, Kate Herbert."

Damien rolled his eyes and shook his head.

"That case is closed, Detective," he sighed. "My wife committed suicide."

"It's been reopened. Some new information has come to light that leads us to believe it might not have been so open-and-shut."

"What information?" Damien tried to strike an arrogant tone, but didn't quite achieve it.

"Why don't we go down to the station to talk about it?" Adams said.

"Why don't you just answer my fucking question?"

There was a brief flash of a sneer on Adams' face. He glanced at the others near the door, then back at Damien.

"Okay, fine. Dr. Taylor has been taken into custody, and has had some interesting things to say. He said that you approached him about getting some sleeping pills for your wife. He thought that was kind of strange since he wasn't your wife's doctor."

"If it was so strange," Damien replied sounding bored, "why did he give me the prescription?"

"Considering the legal shitstorm Dr. Taylor's already going through right now, including the case of your illegal prescription, I don't think you're in a position to slough your blame off onto him. He's answering to plenty of charges already. He saw an opportunity to lessen the charges against himself just a little bit, and he took it. If we had gotten you first, you might have had a chance to do the same, but," he shrugged and left the sentence hanging.

"The next day," Adams continued, "your wife is dead from an overdose of sleeping pills."

Several of those listening from the door gasped in shock.

"He thought that timing seemed a little hinky." Adams raised his eyebrows. "I gotta say I do, too."

Rachel glanced fearfully, questioningly at Suzy. Suzy nodded an affirmation.

"That's all you've got?" Damien asked belligerently. "The coincidental timing of her suicide? That's completely circumstantial. You have no proof that I had anything to do with it."

"That's not entirely true," Suzy said. "I saw it."

Adams turned to Suzy, his eyebrows rising even higher.

"And who are you?"

"Suzy MacKinley."

"Don't listen to her," Damien spat, "she's just a fucking self-proclaimed spirit medium."

"Excuse me, Damien," Rachel snapped, "but isn't that what you are?"

"What did you see, Ms. MacKinley?" Adams asked.

Suzy looked at Adams for a moment. She threw a glance at Damien and Rachel, then back at Adams, realizing the chances were good that he wouldn't believe her.

What the hell, she thought.

"I was communicating with Kate, whose spirit is still here in this house. She allowed me to see what happened to her. Damien crushed a few sleeping pills and put them in her sandwich. After she was too sleepy to think clearly or to fight back, he gave her more."

Suzy knew her expectation was correct as Adams was frowning and squinting at her in total disbelief. Damien was smiling as if he knew that he had just proved his point about her.

"A ghost told you this?" Adams asked.

"That's right," Suzy replied firmly.

"Okay," Adams said somewhat dismissively, "if we need any more information about that, we'll get in touch." He turned back to Damien. "In the meantime, Mr. Specter, why don't we go down to the station."

"Am I under arrest?"

"Not yet."

He looked pointedly at Damien and motioned toward the two uniformed officers. Damien sighed in disgust and walked toward the officers, shaking his head, as the crowd parted for them.

"I'll be right behind you," Adams said, and the officers nodded in response. Some of the people followed to watch Damien being escorted out, while a few stayed at the door.

Adams turned back to Suzy.

"Okay, Ms. MacKinley, I'm not saying I believe your ghost story, but I'd be remiss if I didn't follow up on those marks on your throat."

"Damien did that," she replied, putting a hand up to her neck. "He tried to strangle me after he found out what I had seen."

Adams looked around at Rachel and James, who were still standing near Suzy. They both nodded.

Adams peered more closely at James.

"You're the camera man, aren't you?"

"That's right," James said.

"Yeah, my wife likes your show," Adams continued. "I've seen it a couple of times."

He looked at Suzy and back at James.

"I don't suppose you got that on film, did you?"

"Only the beginning," James replied. "I put the camera down when Damien started choking Suzy. I couldn't be one of those assholes who shoots video of some horrendous event just so they can get a cool video without lifting a finger to help."

"Hmm," Adams frowned.

"But this camera," James continued, pointing to the stationary camera, "has been rolling for hours. The video downloads into a bank of hard drives over there." He pointed a few feet away from the camera.

"Okay," Adams nodded. "I'm going to need that footage." He looked back at Suzy. "Even if I can't prove Specter's involvement in his wife's murder, I can charge him with your attempted murder."

Adams suddenly shivered violently as the temperature abruptly dropped in their vicinity. As he did, a white stream of swirling vapor appeared to pass directly through his body, mixing with the quivering cloud of his exhalation.

The cloud coalesced into the image of a woman standing directly in front of him.

A gasp sounded from the people lingering near the doorway.

"Oh my god," James breathed, "Kate!"

She looked at James and, despite the cold temperature, she smiled warmly at him. Then, she turned toward Adams.

Adams' head whipped around toward James, then back to Kate, his eyes twice their usual size.

"You're Katherine Herbert?" he whispered.

She nodded. A few seconds passed before Adams could speak again.

"Did your husband murder you?"

Again, Kate nodded. Adams swallowed and shivered again, as the apparition gradually dissipated into vapor once more, and faded from view.

As the temperature rose, Adams shivered again and looked at James.

"Please tell me the camera got that."

James looked at the camera and saw the red light was still on. He nodded,

"One of the first outcomes we won't have to enhance with special effects," James mused.

» § «

After getting the most recent hard drive from James, and taking down contact information for him, Suzy and Rachel, Detective Adams left. James told the lingering production staff to go home.

Feeling emotionally exhausted, he plopped down into the chair next to Damien's. Suzy and Rachel sat on the loveseat, leaving Damien's chair conspicuously empty.

"Hey, what's up?"

They turned toward the door and saw Terry coming into the studio.

"Where the hell have you been?" James asked.

"Well, if you must know, I was in the bathroom." Terry placed a hand on his stomach. "Those spicy breakfast burritos didn't sit very well with me."

He looked around at the otherwise empty room.

"What did I miss?"

od, I feel so stupid!" Rachel said. "You and Fin saw what he was like right from the start."

"Well, to be fair," Suzy replied, "all we saw was a creepy, slimy, shifty bamboozler. We didn't see the murderous side of him."

Rachel rolled her eyes, but she managed a smile to show Suzy there were no hard feelings.

"How do you think I feel?" James asked. "I've known him for years, and I never saw that side of him."

"I guess he was good at hiding what he didn't want others to see," Terry contributed. He had obliviously plopped down into the central chair. The others didn't bother asking him to move.

"Yeah," Suzy agreed, "I suppose so."

"Sorry if this is TMI," Rachel said, cringing a bit, "but one of the things that creeps me out the most is remembering sleeping with Damien while his murdered wife's ghost was in the house." She looked at Suzy. "I wonder why she didn't attack me while I was here."

"Indiscriminately vengeful ghosts, I've found, are mainly the product of TV shows and movies," Suzy replied. "I've seen them to be much more discerning. They're just the spiritual continuation of what they were like as humans.

"In Kate's case, she knew Damien was a philanderer, and that's part of what moved her to kick him out of here in the first place. She likely didn't blame you.

"Also, she had heard Damien talk about the idea of calling in a priest to do an exorcism. She didn't know how effective that would be against her, but she probably realized that renewing her physical assaults would reopen that possibility, and she didn't want to endanger her ability to watch over her daughters."

"Oh my god," Rachel said, pressing a hand to her chest, tears coming to her eyes, "those poor girls! What's going to happen to them?"

"I'll look after them," James said. "That was going to be the plan anyway, after today."

Rachel cast a warm, grateful look at him.

"So, were you not going to bother letting me know it's all over?"

Suzy looked up at Fin as he came in with Julie in the baby carrier.

"Oh," she said, putting her head back and sighing heavily, "sorry, Fin. It seems there have been some developments."

» § «

"So," Fin said, sitting across from Suzy, "you saw the entire range of his life, from infantile to adultery."

Suzy smiled, as she often did, at Fin's wordsmithing. She was sitting on the loveseat, nursing Julie, a thin blanket draped over her shoulder.

"Yeah, he wasn't quite the shining paragon of virtue that he wanted others to see."

She frowned.

"I have to say, though, that this case feels kind of anticlimactic."

"Really?" Fin asked.

"He was so worked up about this demon haunting him, and trying to get us involved, for whatever reason, but it turned out to just be his dead wife."

"His *murdered* wife," Fin emphasized. "And you caught the murderer. I wouldn't call that an anticlimax."

"Yeah, I guess," Suzy conceded.

"Anyway, I think I can confidently say that Julie and I are glad you're okay."

Fin could hear the sound of Julie sucking under the blanket, at the same time that his own stomach growled. He looked over at the food table.

"So, is anybody going to do anything about that leftoverfest?"

"I think it's up to you," Suzy said.

"If there are any breakfast burritos left," Terry added, "I'd be careful about those."

"Noted," Fin replied as he stood up and walked over toward the catering table.

Rachel still sat next to Suzy, although she was now leaning against her, her head on Suzy's shoulder. She seemed dazed.

"You're gonna be okay, sweetie," Suzy said.

"I know," Rachel agreed. "I've got you. You're just about *all* I have."

"Hey," Suzy said in a tough-sounding voice, "I'm a lot!"

"You are," Rachel smiled. She sighed, then she frowned. "I'm hungry, though. I haven't eaten anything since this morning."

"You better hurry before Fin gets finished with it."

Rachel smiled again, and she kissed Suzy on the cheek. She stood up and walked toward the food table.

James watched Rachel go. Rachel bent over the table next to Fin, and Fin briefly draped an arm sympathetically around her shoulders.

James tentatively made his way toward the loveseat, sitting down next to Suzy, careful to not look too closely at what she was doing.

"You're a good friend of Rachel's, aren't you?" he asked.

"I am," Suzy replied, looking over her shoulder at her friend picking through the catering selections. "She's pretty much the best person I know. Well, maybe next to Fin."

"Yeah," James said, looking down at his hands. He frowned as he regarded his entwined fingers.

"What is it, James?" Suzy asked.

He looked up at her, obviously uneasy about something. His frown deepened, and he glanced over his shoulder at Rachel, then back down at his hands. A few seconds passed before he found his words.

"I've liked her from the moment I met her but — well, she was involved with Damien who, it turns out, was a major asshole, to say the least."

He looked back up at Suzy.

"Do you think she — I mean, would she consider — is there any chance she might — "

"James," Suzy said in a tone that indicated she was putting him out of his misery, "all you can do is ask."

She glanced over her shoulder again at Rachel.

"Maybe give her a few minutes, though."

James smiled and nodded.

"I do know," Suzy added, "she's recently made her house more child friendly."

Notes and Acknowledgments

We introverted creative types can be a sensitive lot. We need encouragement and confirmation that what we're doing really is as good as we think it is. Sometimes we need oh-so-gentle critiques and suggestions to make what we're doing better. My wife, Linda, does this so well, helping me keep my work on track, while keeping my self-esteem intact. Being a creative type herself, I can only hope that whatever support *I* provide is as helpful to her.

Also, readers are essential to a writer. You're now one of those, and, I'm pleased to note, you're next in line. Pass it along. Tell others what you think of it. Who knows, you might be the one to spread the infection and get this story into the general populace.

I sometimes get positive personal feedback, and I'm not going to downplay that at all. It's always very nice. But it doesn't spread the word. **If you like what you've read, please consider leaving a brief review at Amazon and/or Goodreads.**